BLACK BULLET

THE BULLET THAT CHANGED THE WORLD

7

SHIDEN KANZAKI

ILLUSTRATION BY
SAKI UKAI

"My name is Enju Aihara... I'm transferring into this school because of my parents. It's good to meet you."

"I am not."

BLACK BULLET 7
CONTENTS

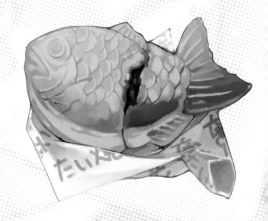

BLACK★BULLET

THE BULLET THAT CHANGED THE WORLD

7

SHIDEN KANZAKI

ILLUSTRATION BY SAKI UKAI

YEN ON
NEW YORK

BLACK BULLET, Volume 7
SHIDEN KANZAKI

Translation by Kevin Gifford
Cover art by Saki Ukai

BLACK BULLET, Volume 7
©SHIDEN KANZAKI 2014
All rights reserved.
Edited by ASCII MEDIA WORKS
First published in Japan in 2014 by KADOKAWA CORPORATION, Tokyo.

English translation rights arranged with KADOKAWA CORPORATION, Tokyo,
through Tuttle-Mori Agency, Inc., Tokyo.

Yen On
1290 Avenue of the Americas
New York, NY 10104

Visit us at yenpress.com
facebook.com/yenpress
twitter.com/yenpress
yenpress.tumblr.com
instagram.com/yenpress

First Yen On Edition: September 2017

Yen On is an imprint of Yen Press, LLC.
The Yen On name and logo are trademarks of Yen Press, LLC.

Library of Congress Cataloging-in-Publication Data
Names: Kanzaki, Shiden, author. | Gifford, Kevin, translator. | Ukai, Saki, illustrator.
Title: Black bullet. Volume 7, The bullet that changed the world / Shiden Kanzaki ;
illustrations by Saki Ukai ; translation by Kevin Gifford.
Other titles: The bullet that changed the world
Description: New York, NY : Yen On, 2017. | Series: Black bullet ; 7
Identifiers: LCCN 2015046479 | ISBN 9780316304993 (v. 1 : pbk.) |
ISBN 9780316344890 (v. 2 : pbk.) | ISBN 9780316344906 (v. 3 : pbk.) |
ISBN 9780316344913 (v. 4 : pbk.) | ISBN 9780316344920 (v. 5 : pbk.) |
ISBN 9780316344944 (v. 6 : pbk.) | ISBN 9780316510646 (v. 7 : pbk.)
Subjects: | CYAC: Science fiction. | BISAC: FICTION /
Science Fiction / Adventure.
Classification: LCC PZ7.1.K29 Blac 2016 | DDC [Fic]—dc23
LC record available at http://lccn.loc.gov/2015046479

ISBNs: 978-0-316-51064-6 (paperback)
978-0-316-44200-8 (ebook)

1 3 5 7 9 10 8 6 4 2

LSC-C

Printed in the United States of America

PROLOGUE   THE KING OF PLAGUES

Liquid poured from the fountain, around the statue of some god or another. It took in some blue from the sky as it fell and wafted the crisp smell of fresh water into the nostrils of passersby as it broke the surface of the collection pool.

It drove the woman in white to bend a knee, remove one of her long gloves, and slowly plunge her hand inside. It felt good; the cold water was comfortable in the midsummer heat. As she knelt, she could see the corroded aluminum of single-yen coins and the rusted copper of ten-yen pieces that had sunk to the bottom.

Letting her mind go as she flicked her wrist around, the woman could feel all the dust and muck from the world around her vanish into thin air. But the serenity didn't last long. She heard heavy footsteps on the stone pavement behind her.

"It is time, Lady Seitenshi."

"Have you figured out where the Neck and Solomon's Ring are yet, Kikunojo?" asked the Seitenshi, the head of government in Tokyo Area, as she turned around.

The chief aide's face didn't move a single muscle. "We are currently searching for it, my lady."

"Have you discussed things with Satomi yet?"

"If I could say so, my lady, I am against entrusting any of that to him in the first place."

The Seitenshi rose and surveyed the large, gray-haired man behind her, just in time to see him finally drop his brows a little. "Would it be overstepping my bounds," she said, "to ask why?"

"My lady, he is merely a civsec officer. You are granting him far too much responsibility."

"You're certain that Andrei Litvintsev and his people have entered Tokyo Area?"

"We are certain, yes."

She let out a sigh. "Not exactly a rosy future, is it?"

"We had best focus on the summit ahead of us first."

"......"

"Less than enthusiastic, my lady?"

The Seitenshi closed her eyes for a moment before slowly opening them.

"Let's get going."

She followed Kikunojo across the stepping stones. They strode through a tree-lined, well-manicured lawn, up to a roaring wall of water. The moment she stood in front of it, the water flow stopped dead, a combination of face-detecting sensors and actuators bringing a corridor into view.

Passing through a damp, square gazebo and an artificial waterfall on the other side, she found herself holding her hat down fast against a brisk side wind. All she could hear was the rustling grass under her feet as she looked up from under her hat, regarding a chalk-white building looming under the clear blue sky.

This was Akasaka Palace, the government's guest house and reception hall for official ceremonies. It had been heavily refurbished after the Gastrea War, but the off-white granite and pondering sense of symmetry remained just as it was in its 1909 opening.

Proceeding past the security guards in black and through the front door, the Seitenshi was met with a room laden with décor just as intricate and gaudy as her own palace. An attendant guided them to the mighty door that opened the way to the White Phoenix Room.

"It's now or never, my lady."

The Seitenshi felt the sweat on her palms through the gloves. She could palpably feel her pulsing heart through her crossed arms.

"…What happens beyond these doors could change the entire future of Tokyo Area, couldn't it?"

Don't let your guard down, she told herself. *You're dealing with people incredibly gifted at making others slip up—with the extensive experience required to freely wield that talent, no less.*

She took a deep breath and started to open the door. It made more of a heavy thudding sound than she expected, enough to make the conversation beyond skid to a halt as the people inside turned their eyes to her at once. She didn't flinch. That much, at least, she was expecting.

The room, modeled after what the late-era French royal family preferred in the eighteenth century, was thrown into a chest-splitting silence. There was a fresco on the ceiling, the curtains lined with gold fiber. It was uniformly laid out in off-white and golden colors, topped off with a grandiose, 800-kilogram chandelier that shone so brightly, it was hard to look at directly.

The Seitenshi walked up to her appointed desk. Kikunojo pulled out the chair for her as she sat.

"Were you out picking flowers, Lady Seitenshi?"

A jab at her for being a woman, perhaps. It was painfully difficult to retain a cool face against such a malignant joke.

"I apologize for being late, President Saitake. Please continue."

Sougen Saitake, head of Osaka Area and a man whose face eternally evoked that of a lion in midpounce, gave an embarrassed grimace and snorted, as if he was the one being affronted. As he did, the Seitenshi surveyed the collection of elderly men surrounding her, and let out a little sigh at their eminent-looking visages. They were all seated in one room: the leaders of the Osaka, Sendai, Hakata, and Hokkaido Areas.

A historic moment—the first official summit between all five heads of state in the islands of Japan.

It was sort of like a G5 summit that Japan had all to itself. One had to wonder how apt that comparison was, but Tokyo Area's responsibilities as host were still nothing to gloss over.

"Now, can we get back to the Japanese national flag issue, *please*?"

The voice, accompanied by a rapping on the table, came from what the Seitenshi was pretty sure was the Hakata—

"Which issue is this, Prime Minister Kaihoko?"

There were deep lines drawn across the dark, tanned skin of Masamori Kaihoko, prime minister of the southern-lying Hakata Area. His hair was a salt-and-pepper mix, and his deep-set, heavy eyebrows only added to the physical threat he exuded whenever he spoke.

"Right now," Kaihoko huffily began, "Japan is still using the red-and-white *hinomaru* as its official flag, but it's been taking a beating in my native Area. People say the red circle resembles the eye of a Gastrea too much. What I'm suggesting is that we change it—change it to anything, really. A yellow circle, a black one, whatever."

"Well, make it a black circle, then," the man sitting next to him said as he nodded amicably. "As a Varanium-producing Area, a black circle would represent what we're all about perfectly."

This was the newly appointed prime minister of the Hokkaido Area to the north. He enjoyed nervously fussing with his monocle whenever he spoke, a rather distinct five-o'clock shadow of a mustache encircling his lips.

The suggestion was not one the Seitenshi was willing to let slide. "Prime Minister Juzouji," she said, "I think we should consider the role of tradition here. There is intense meaning, after all, to the things our ancestors helped protect for us."

"So, you're telling me to ignore the will of my constituency?"

The Seitenshi turned to Kaihoko. "Yes," she began, "I know you're up for election soon, Mr. Kaihoko. But focusing on the day-to-day whims of the people will leave your administration rudderless. A successful government needs to run on guiding principles, lest it run the risk of losing its mandate to lead."

The head of Hakata Area closed his opened jaw tightly, raising an eyebrow in rage.

"Damn it, girl…"

"I'm glad we have an understanding," the Seitenshi calmly replied to the heedless name-calling. Maybe this *was* working her way. Maybe she had what it took to fend off Kaihoko and Juzouji—these weather-beaten career politicians—after all.

Saitake raised a bony hand, sneering at the others in his room. "Let me weigh in, then," he rasped. "I wanted to ask about the Cassiopeia Project..."

"Yes," the Seitenshi instantly replied. "I would like to see work proceed as quickly as possible on that."

She was expecting this to come up. Cassiopeia involved building a vast underground rail network, using gigantic tunnel-boring machines to link the five Areas together. It was a central part of the Seitenshi's political platform, and it was a project she fervently wanted to see take root, no matter how much political capital it took.

"An underground network"—she spoke clearly as she sized up her peers one by one—"will not only energize the economies of all five of our Areas; it will also serve as a symbol of peace and harmony between us. It will kindle a new, and substantial, light of hope within our people—the hope that mankind is capable of striking back against the Gastrea menace."

"Oh, I don't know about that..."

A shiver ran down the Seitenshi's spine as a subdued voice spoke up for the first time. It came from the prime minister of Sendai Area: His hair was completely white, right down to the eyebrows, and it had receded to the point where it existed only in a pair of tufts around his ears. It made the top of his head shine, like he had oiled it before coming in. The combination of protruding cheekbones and small, beady eyes gave him a gorillalike appearance, and his eyes shone with what seemed like a deep suspicion of everyone and everything around him.

It was enough to make her unconsciously straighten her posture. That took a lot. She was in the same room with Sougen Saitake, a man whom she was fairly certain had tried to kill her not long ago; Masamori Kaihoko, every bit Saitake's equal when it came to extreme beliefs and aggressive politics; and Tsukihiko Juzouji, still a complete question mark when it came to his abilities as head of state. But it was Muramaro Ino, prime minister of Sendai Area, whom the Seitenshi considered to be the eye of this typhoon that the summit was shaping up to be.

"By which I mean," Ino muttered, putting heavy emphasis on each syllable, "that it is simply not realistic. How much time and money do you think that would require? Perhaps *you* have the financial freedom for it, Lady Seitenshi, but we might all be old and senile by the time they hold the ribbon-cutting ceremony."

It seemed he meant to get a laugh out of the last sentence. But in the heavy-handed atmosphere, it never had a chance.

"Prime Minister Ino, I don't know if you've been following recent advances in tunnel development, but the progress they've been making is simply astonishing. If we could deploy shield machines in Tokyo Area and Sendai Area, we could create a true physical link between the two Areas far more quickly than you'd think."

"Mm, yes," Ino responded leisurely as he scratched his head. Her argument, as she feared, had fallen on deaf ears.

Linking all five Areas together by rail would drastically reduce transport costs. It would also take Hokkaido Area's inexpensive agricultural produce, Osaka Area's heavy-industry manufacturing, and Tokyo Area's world-leading Varanium supply and collate them together into a united front for Japanese trade.

She was sure Sendai Area's farmers and manufacturers were lobbying Ino against the idea. The think tanks that had Ino's ear were similarly interested in protecting their vested interests, no doubt.

In a way, the Seitenshi couldn't help but smile to herself at the irony. As recently as ten years ago, there was just a single nation known as Japan; now, in 2031, it was hard to picture reunification happening anytime soon. But that was what she wanted to see in her lifetime—five Areas returning to one and resurrecting the country of Japan. Right now, however, she suspected that Gastrea weren't necessarily the greatest obstacle after all.

In the end, and no doubt to Ino's great relief, no agreement was made on the Cassiopeia Project. It was delayed again, and the Seitenshi would have to settle for that. The other heads of state agreed it was too early to decide on everything in this meeting, that they needed to bring the proposal back home for deliberation. But if these old men didn't have the discretionary power to act on the idea, who else in their governments would?

It wasn't until the group began to wrap up their discussions, which touched on everything from macroeconomics to energy and climate-change issues, that the taciturn Ino decided to speak up.

"By the way..."

—Maybe he had picked this exact moment to speak, once everyone had started to soften their stances a little.

"I understand Tokyo Area possesses something called the Inheritance of the Seven Stars."

The Seitenshi's eyelids burst wide open. She exchanged glances with Kikunojo, standing next to her.

"Where did you hear about this 'Inheritance'?"

"Well," Ino said with a gloom-inducing laugh, "I *do* have something like an information agency at my disposal. It's just idle gossip, I imagine, but according to the chatter that's been related to me, Tokyo Area is allegedly using a mysterious object known as the Inheritance of the Seven Stars as a catalyst to summon a Stage Five Gastrea—a Zodiac. There's no truth to it, is there?"

"I can't answer that," the Seitenshi said curtly.

Ino's eyes glinted with suspicion. "What does *that* reply mean, I wonder? There's no need for constraint. It would be perfectly fine to laugh it off as the idle gossip that it is."

"I can't answer that."

"Well! So now the leader professing to be the great uniter of the five Areas is hiding things from the rest of us?"

The Seitenshi was at a loss for an answer. She knew this was bad. She was concocting a situation for herself where she was all but inviting her peers to interrogate her.

"I apologize, but this is conflicting with Tokyo Area classified material."

Her voice held none of the calm coolness from before, nor was there even the slightest indication a reply would do anything to soothe the supreme awkwardness of the room. But, mercifully, Ino did not pursue her any further. The summit came to a close—one where they had failed to find a compromise on nearly every topic.

But in the space of just a few days, the discord between the two would trigger events potent enough to change the world.

"Keep your hands moving! Get back to your posts!"

The shouting from the field boss echoed across the cavern, almost physically driving him to take up the grip of the jackhammer and drive the chisel down into the hard rock beneath. He pushed the throttle lever, and the resulting pneumatic action battered the hammer's Varanium chisel into the rock. The overpowering earthen smell in the air, combined with the bone-rattling jackhammer recoil, made him instinctively keep one eye shut.

A dank, humid underground cavern was never an ideal work environment. The man found himself regularly lowering the hammer grip just so he could wipe the sweat from his brow. All around him, under the dim light of a bare bulb, other hammerers, faces dirty with thick, heavy dust, were loading crushed rock into a conveyor. From here, in this pit, it wasn't clear whether it was afternoon or evening.

To Hitoshi Kamisu, it felt like he had taken his life and tossed it right into an antlion pit.

He was inside one of the mines that dotted the Unexplored Territory beyond the Monoliths. Before the Gastrea War broke out in 2021, he was importing and selling cosmetics to people. That evaporated quickly, and in the Gastrea-infested postwar era, where all aircraft were required by law to have civsec-piloted escort planes to protect them from bird- and insect-type Gastrea, the resulting costs no longer made the risk/reward ratio at all feasible.

Back in college, Hitoshi read somewhere—maybe from Darwin, but maybe not—that "It is not the strongest of the species that survives, nor the most intelligent; it is the one that is most adaptable to change." Along those lines, Japan in the postwar years, so drastically changed in every way by the Gastrea, was nothing he was capable of adapting to. He had more than enough money in the bank to reestablish himself, but something made him too timid to try much of anything anymore. Instead of taking risks and challenging himself to new heights, he was perfectly happy to cruise along and watch his finances gradually dwindle.

Rock bottom didn't come along until ten or so years later. He was more or less kidnapped by yakuza seeking redress for some financial debts. That was the beginning of Hitoshi Kamisu, Varanium miner. It was simple, brain-dead work, nothing with any discernible future potential to it.

B3F, the assigned floor Hitoshi had descended to in the mine elevator, was both darker and gradually narrower the deeper it went. The iron beams supporting the ceiling were nothing he felt safe counting on. A coworker told him that modern technology had all but eliminated cave-ins, but this operation was an illegal one—unauthorized mining run by a front firm for the yakuza—so there was no telling how much of this "technology" was up to code.

He was shaken out of bed each morning, fed a breakfast that was never particularly good, then forced to work until evening before he collapsed back into his shabby blankets. Anything that could give him the current time, like a watch or cell phone, had been confiscated from him first thing, so it was hard to know for sure, but his body clock told him it was between one and two in the afternoon.

The thing that really exasperated him about this job was how it took a good hundred kilograms of ore to extract a single Troy ounce (around thirty-one grams, apparently) of Varanium. It was his job to hammer through all that ore.

On more than a few occasions, he found himself jerked out of bed after having dreams of Gastrea screaming at him in deep, hoarse cries. Civsecs were handling security duty here 24-7, but the kind of civsecs the yakuza dug up weren't much more than criminals themselves—birds of a feather, and all that. Their job seemed to be less security and more about rounding up miners who went AWOL. And besides, the miners here all had money troubles with the yakuza. They all knew, should a powerful Gastrea come strolling along, the yakuza sure as hell weren't gonna spend any *more* money rescuing their asses.

"Yo! How many times I gotta tell you? Keep your hands moving!"

Hitoshi grunted to himself and returned to work.

A shuddering boom sent the light bulb flickering as pebbles and dust shook free from the ceiling. Waves of surprise ensued from the miners. Hitoshi thought it was some kind of controlled blasting work, but another faraway *boom* made dust fall from above again. Cold sweat ran down his arms, his heart racing. He didn't like this.

The sound gradually grew to a rhythm. By the seventh time, the boom was close enough to trigger earthquakelike shaking. Hitoshi fell, his legs going out from under him as his hip painfully struck the floor. It was coming closer. It was almost like—

"Are those some kind of footsteps...?"

The words, muttered to no one in particular, were like a seed of anxiety planting itself in his heart. It sprouted in an instant, with vines of terror entwining his body. Before anyone could even shout "Run!" he was already in action. The field boss was screaming at everyone to return to their posts, but Hitoshi knew his heart wasn't in it. The managers were outnumbered, and they had no motive to fend back the oncoming rush of bodies.

The mine elevator, packed to the gills with people surrounding him, shook as it emitted ominous, shrill creaking sounds, like fingernails on a chalkboard. The hardy miners onboard all cringed, fearful of a ceiling collapse. What *was* this? What was going on?

Soon, the car made it to ground level. The fence surrounding it was quickly swept away. Hiroshi jumped over to the frame of the nearby hoisting tower, groaning at the sharp light piercing his vision—it must have been afternoon after all.

But the next moment, everything went dark as the sun disappeared. Hitoshi looked up at the sky, unsure of what had happened.

And then he saw it—

It made his sense of scale go haywire. That was the only way to put it. From his post in the hoisting tower, he was looking at a long, thin, rippling pile of muscle. Legs lined both sides of its body, each one bursting with bristles and wartlike growths. This thing was right in front of Hitoshi, and to him, it was a majestic sight—one that seemed to make all descriptions of hugeness obsolete.

The long, vertical body, reminiscent of the Great Wall of China, looked like some kind of ringed worm or leech. Its body was upright, its ground-driven legs divided into segments. The more developed of these legs curved outward like scythes while the bottommost ones dug into the earth. It was a mammoth-level Gastrea, and it was right in the midst of crossing over Hitoshi's hoisting tower. Its stomach portion blocked the sun and scared him out of his wits.

With a mixture of screaming and shouting, the security civsecs fled the scene in all directions, fully abandoning the mine site. And with every step the Gastrea took, Hitoshi's stomach was jostled and torn by the vibration of the boom. It sent plumes of rock dust flying into the air as it smashed through the portable Monoliths lining the site, chopping them to pieces like a karate demonstration.

Then Hitoshi noticed the large number of saclike growths on the bottom half of the Gastrea. They looked like eggs, and something about them triggered a memory.

"Viral sacs? No...no way."

He groaned and took a step back.

The Zodiac Gastrea, king of all Gastreas—

"Libra, the King of Plagues...!"

There was no doubt about it. It was one of the creatures that made the entire world shudder ten years ago.

Two hours later, the news had made its way to the nerve center of Tokyo Area—the Seitenshi's palace in District 1.

The office in the western tower, used by the head of state, was tense. Staffers ran to and fro, confirming sources and trying to figure out a response.

"So, Libra halted its advance at that mine," the Seitenshi stated calmly, elbows on an enormous work desk. "Where is it?"

Kikunojo, face stern as always, waved a hand. The room darkened, revealing a large holopanel map hovering in midair. It showed a large stretch of Unexplored Territory between the Tokyo and Sendai Areas.

"It sits nearby the Mount Nasu range, in what we would've called Tochigi Prefecture ten years ago. We don't have any record of the government awarding mining rights in the area, so it was probably an illegal operation."

The Seitenshi stared intently at the holodisplay as it shone in the darkness.

"...So Libra appeared near the midpoint between Tokyo and Sendai. What's its status?"

"Currently, it has taken up position directly above the mine, coiled like a snake."

"So it's stopped moving?"

Kikunojo shook his head. "That I cannot say."

"What was Libra's ability again...?"

"The ability to take in tens of thousands of viri, fatal exclusively to human beings, and diffuse them into the air. These viri are not only breathable; they can be absorbed through the upper skin layer. You would need the latest in anti-contamination suits to physically block them. The viri Libra produces are also resistant to ultraviolet light and can make it through the Monolith magnetic field. It went through Russia ten years ago and turned that place into a living hell. The streets were filled with people dying of all kinds of bizarre, unheard-of, and agonizing diseases. The stench of the bodies reportedly made it all the way to Beijing."

"Hence 'the King of Plagues,' I suppose. So what about the viral sacs around its stomach?"

"They are active, my lady."

"Get our analysts to figure out when it'll release its viral load."

"Yes, my lady. Although judging by its abilities, I'd say Sendai Area has more to be concerned about than we do."

"How so?"

"It'll catch a ride on the westerly winds."

The Seitenshi brought a startled hand to her lips.

"Ah, have you already noticed? If Libra releases its viral load at its current location…the weather will have an effect on it, but it's all but guaranteed to follow the prevailing winds and make a direct hit on Sendai Area."

"Well, there's practically no chance of defeating a Zodiac with normal weapons. I only hope Sendai doesn't get panicky and start firing missiles at it."

The Seitenshi turned toward a policy secretary next to her.

"Tell Prime Minister Ino that we're counting on him to make the right decisions."

"Reporting, sirs!" Suddenly, another secretary burst through the door, panting.

"What is it?"

"Prime Minister Ino has occupied the Tokyo Area embassy in Sendai Area and is presently holding our ambassador! He's closed off the airports and canceled all flights going to or from Tokyo!"

The Seitenshi felt as though someone had struck her in the face with a hammer. She found herself flying up from her seat.

"What are you…talking about?"

"Sendai Area's claiming that we used our Inheritance of the Seven Stars to summon Libra in order to destroy them. They're asking us repeatedly to withdraw Libra at once. They're reporting it on TV, too. Look!"

The aide breathlessly brought up a command on the holodisplay. He didn't even have to change the channel before Prime Minister Ino appeared, standing behind a lectern and shaking his fist in the air.

"Ladies and gentlemen of Sendai Area! As all of you know, our homeland, which was ravaged in the Gastrea War ten years ago, has restored itself to good health thanks to the efforts of every man, woman, and child in this Area. Those efforts are why the United Nations has recognized us as the sovereign nation that we are. But now, the rights we fought so hard for—the right to sovereignty, and to our continued existence—are under mortal threat."

His eyes, hidden under the drooping flaps on his forehead, suddenly shot open as he rapped at the lectern.

"That threat is none other than Tokyo Area! Our intelligence services have discovered that Tokyo is concealing a new technology that enables them to control Zodiac Gastrea at will."

"That's not true!" shouted the Seitenshi, even though she knew it was pointless. "The Inheritance doesn't have that kind of power!"

"In other words, Sendai Area's life-or-death situation at the hands of Libra is entirely due to the machinations of the Tokyo Area government. No matter what their intentions are, good or bad, it is clear they have crossed a line no government should ever cross. Thus, we have been forced to take retaliatory measures against the Seitenshi administration in Tokyo in order to defuse this Libra threat. What I am asking you for, citizens of Sendai Area, is—"

That was all she could stand. She waved the panel shut and hung her head low, shaking it softly. An all-penetrating silence enveloped the office.

…He was asking for war. All-out war between the Areas. That was what was on her, and everyone else's, mind.

The Seitenshi weakly raised her head, drawing the attention of the rest of her staff. They were patiently awaiting her orders.

She fingered the rosary around her neck. Its solid feel between her fingers was the only solace her heart could reach. She took a deep breath.

"We need to release a statement denying all involvement immediately."

"Will they believe us?"

"The longer we delay, the guiltier we'll look to them. Also, we'll need to send a special envoy over to Sendai in secret."

One of the ministry secretaries gave her a nervous glance. "Would this be a good time to disclose the existence of the Inheritance to the other Areas, do you think?"

"No. Even if we tell all four other Areas about it, I doubt we can expect them to use it in a peaceful manner. And with things as bad as they are now, I doubt Sendai Area would believe much of what we told them. The ideal solution would be to take out Libra with our own forces, but…"

The secretary adjusted his glasses and brought his eyes down upon the documents in front of him.

"…But if we could do that, we would've done it ten years ago, I suppose. Libra's evolved from the DNA of hundreds of thousands of species. Its multi-layered shell can withstand all types of modern weaponry. The only really effective offense we have on hand is nuclear, I think, but…"

"…No," the Seitenshi promptly interrupted. "It might be Unexplored Territory now, but using nuclear weapons in former Japanese territory would violate the New World Treaty."

An analyst entered the room with an "excuse me" and spoke into the ear of a secretary, who then nodded.

"The lab's done with its results. If the viral sacs continue to grow at their current speed, they'll start to be released five days from now. Sendai Area also sent us a final bulletin indicating that they'll attack us if Libra isn't recalled within four days."

"Four days…"

The clock began to tick in the minds of everyone on hand.

"We'll need to start figuring out ways to reconcile with them and eliminate Libra right away. If we don't do something, this hate's just going to cover the entire world."

"Lady Seitenshi…"

Turning around, she saw Kikunojo, his eyes now open after an extended period of being closed. They shone coldly, disturbingly so.

"We must isolate the Sendai Area ambassador in his embassy and prepare a retaliation immediately."

The Seitenshi quietly shook her head.

"We cannot. If hate continues to breed hate, it will lead us all down to hell before long. This whole case might be connected to Solomon's Ring and the Neck, as well..."

"My lady, is there *any* point in discussing that with things as they are right now?" The gray-haired man's half-shouted question cowed the other staffers into submission. Silence returned once more.

"My lady," Kikunojo continued after a moment, voice clearer, "Sendai Area has taken our innocent ambassador hostage and turned their missiles toward us. This is going to enrage our people, and that's going to turn their minds toward choosing war. If we don't prepare for that, they'll call us cowards and probably force you out of office."

"I don't care. If that's what the people want, I will accept it."

"My lady, who besides you could ever serve as Tokyo Area's icon? Why don't you understand that sometimes it's your job to meekly sit on the throne of power? It is for the long-term good of Tokyo Area."

"I'm afraid that, this time at least, I cannot listen to your advice."

She pushed Kikunojo back and was just about to shout some orders at a secretary when she was stopped by Kikunojo's outstretched arm.

"I'm afraid that's not possible."

He motioned a command to his side. Suddenly, a large man in black busted in and held the Seitenshi's arms in place. For a moment, she couldn't comprehend what had happened.

"...What is the meaning of this?"

"Lady Seitenshi, I need you to spend some time resting in your room."

The meaning behind Kikunojo's severe expression suddenly became clear.

"...So this is a coup?"

Kikunojo furrowed his brows, revealing a sad look for the first time.

"During the Cuban missile crisis in 1962, America and the Soviet Union had enough nuclear weapons to destroy the world seven and a half times over. Every one of those was aimed at each other, and at the height of the crisis, the fingers were absolutely on the buttons, my lady. Soviet secretary Khrushchev ultimately accepted US negotiators and kept the world from experiencing full nuclear war. He made the right decision for himself, but it made him weak in the eyes of his own people. It became one of the main reasons why he was deposed not long after. You need to remember, Lady Seitenshi, that sometimes the 'correct' decision needs to be dismissed from your mind. I was tasked by the previous Seitenshi to keep you from being overthrown—it is the sole reason why the decrepit old man you see before you has clung to this position."

"Shame on you! And shame on you for attempting to solve everything through sheer power!"

"No one can measure whether a decision is wise or poor. Not even the history books."

"It'll become clear when you rise from your grave and the angel judges you for heaven or hell."

"So be it. If hell wants me, I'm ready to accept it... Take her away."

"I can walk by myself," snapped the Seitenshi as the guard in black shuffled her along. She looked at Kikunojo for another moment or two before turning around and leaving the office.

The light from the three-pronged candlestick warmly flickered, transforming the darkness-enshrouded hallways into a world of sanity and logic.

She never liked the palace at night. Especially in areas without any people around.

Kiyomi Kase, the sole woman among the small army of governmental aides who called the palace home, nervously paced the hall. The painting of a beautiful woman on the wall, created by some famous artist, seemed alive in the darkness, as if waiting for the observer to turn away from her.

Her duty as an aide had kept her at work for nearly the entire previous week, and the amount of work she had today indicated the palace must be turning upside down. Even now, she could see dazzling light come from the western tower. She doubted it'd ever be shut off tonight.

Compared to that, the Seitenshi's personal chambers on the far edge of the western tower were a sort of fortress of solitude, one that only her personal attendants could ever access.

Kiyomi carried a tray with a steaming bowl of soup and bread. With the Seitenshi under house arrest, the lady was stuck in her rooms, forcing Kiyomi to tend to her meals. But she had yet to show any sign of touching them.

Turning her concerns to getting her mistress to eat something for a change, Kiyomi stood in front of the inner door, placed the candlestick down, and knocked a few times.

"Lady Seitenshi, my apologies for bothering you late at night."

She stared at the door, decorated with vinelike curving lines. Only the silence of rejection gave her any reply. She knocked and called her again. But the act was just as futile.

Kiyomi sighed. But just as she turned around to go, she could feel the wind from the other side of the keyhole. She brought a hand to it and waved it against the hole a few times. She wasn't imagining it.

A bad feeling raced across her mind as she called "Excuse me," stuck the correct key in from her ring, and shot through the door.

There was no sign of anyone inside. The silk curtains fluttered in the air. The right-hand curtain had been removed from the rail—and, oddly enough, was nowhere to be seen.

Taking the candlestick out to the balcony, Kiyomi's doubts were answered. The curtain was tied to the handrail outside, flowing listlessly in the wind. She had cut the curtain into strips, then made a rope out of it, one that extended down from the third floor to the ground.

When Kiyomi realized what this meant, she dropped the candlestick, bringing both hands to her mouth.

"Oh my God...!"

BLACK BULLET 7 CHAPTER 01

TOKYO AREA HOLIDAY

1

The edge of the sky had just begun to whiten a bit, the thin veneer of red tightening its grasp over the air before sunrise. The rain from the previous day had collected in puddles in the alley, likewise dampening the trees and delivering much-needed nourishment to the undergrowth below.

To young Rentaro Satomi, this particular commute to school was a bit more stressful than usual. Or maybe that stress was being transmitted to him thanks to the girl in pigtails, standing in front of him with her body turned to look at him.

Enju Aihara tugged at both shoulder straps on the bright red backpack she wore.

"I'm outta here."

Rentaro patted both her shoulders. "One more reminder before you do, Enju. Do *not* use your powers—for any reason. And skip all your gym classes, too. If you ever get a cut or something—"

"'Cover it with your hand and run off somewhere secluded, don't show it healing to anyone,' blah, blah, blah, right? You ever got anything else to say to me?"

"Hmm… All right."

Do I really repeat myself that much? Rentaro wondered. He scratched his head over the thought while Enju gave him a fearless smile. "I'm gonna make it this time, okay?" she declared before whirling her ponytails around and raising her hand in a sharp salute. This didn't exactly put Rentaro at ease, but if Enju was that resolute, there was no point applying further pressure.

Soon, whether she knew about her friend's concerns or not, Enju disappeared into the early-morning mist without another look back.

"Did she go?"

Rentaro turned around to find an attractive young girl in a black school uniform standing in front of the dojo entrance, accompanied by a girl with blonde hair and emerald-green eyes. Apparently they'd just wrapped up morning practice, what with Kisara Tendo wiping the sweat from her still-flushed cheeks with a towel.

"You worried about her?" she asked.

"Not really..." Rentaro looked back toward the mist-laden path that led to Enju's school. "It's more like, 'Good for her to try school again,' you know?"

This seemed to somehow put off Kisara as she gave him a side glance.

"People can't live by themselves, you know. No man is an island."

Rentaro frowned. "Jeez, she's got me, doesn't she?"

It was meant as a show of strength, but then Rentaro realized what it truly was. Here they were, Enju's grand first day of elementary school at a new place, and neither he nor Enju let themselves act like they were enjoying it at all. Was it really something to celebrate, after all, seeing the time come when she finally wiped the dust off that backpack in a corner of her room? Enju had already been driven from one school after being exposed as one of the Cursed Children—and the open-air classroom she attended afterward ended in even more tragic circumstances.

She was cursed, detested. She had every right to wail about her body, to indulge herself in pity. But she didn't.

Rentaro never thought for a moment that he had a decent education. That, on the other hand, was one of Enju's strengths. If there was anything he felt proud about, it was helping her accept herself and access her potential.

All the local schools had worked in tandem with one another to blacklist Enju, so she was traveling to a pretty remote elementary school instead. That was the main reason Enju was up this early—just to travel to class.

"What about you, though, Tina?" Rentaro asked the blonde girl nearby, as she, too, looked down Enju's path.

"I wanna get some more time to think about it, thanks. Including whether I even need school in the first place."

"..."

She had a point. Ten years on from that calamity, in this dying world, was there any real indication in life that going to school and finding a regular job was the right thing to do? It was one of the core questions that tugged at the mind of any man or woman, and Tina was running smack-dab into it. In many ways, it was similar to the emptiness people like Rentaro and Kisara, themselves part of the Stolen Generation, were doomed to grapple with.

There was a small rumbling sound from somewhere. Rentaro stopped. Once he realized it was an airplane engine, he spotted a shining dot in the western skies. As its rumbling grew louder, the dot grew larger and larger; just as it seemed to loom impossibly gigantic above them, the craft zoomed by at supersonic speed, leaving a delayed but surprisingly strong wind behind it.

Rentaro shaded his eyes as he looked up; the nearby trees rustled violently, sending a pile of shredded leaves flying through the air. The dot flew away, fast as ever, and already he had to squint to see it.

"Eesh," Kisara whined as she spat out bits of leaf that went in her mouth. "Are they scrambling *this* early in the morning?"

"That's a supporter fighter from the Tokyo Area force, isn't it? I thought most of 'em got shot down in the Third Kanto Battle."

"They manufactured a bunch more at breakneck speed, I heard. It's still kind of just a staring contest right now, but if it actually gets to be a fight, I don't like our chances all too much. It's hard to imagine we're on equal footing with Sendai right now."

"...You think there'll really be a war?" a concerned Tina asked.

Rentaro was about to say something to reassure her but stopped just before he began. This time, at least, he had no idea how things would turn out.

"They haven't contacted you at all, either, Satomi," a dejected-sounding Kisara said.

Rentaro snorted at the thought. "Why would *my* name come up? There's no room for a civsec in international warfare."

"No, but…like, you've gotten pretty involved in stuff like this over the past little while, so…"

"Yeah, well, it's too complicated this time. Not like the Kanto Battle. If the government needs anybody right now, it's not civsecs. It's diplomats who know how to negotiate."

Rentaro shrugged, only to feel something warm on his palm. The sun was just about ready to peek out above the horizon, its light already making the ground shine.

Kisara clapped her hands, like a teacher asking for her class's attention.

"Well, it's times like these when it's important we stick to the daily routine, all right? We better get ready for school, too. Don't wanna be late!"

2

To Enju Aihara, this new environment felt totally unique, nothing like Magata Elementary School or the open-air classroom. It was a higher-quality school, meant for gifted kids on a college track, so that had something to do with it—but that wasn't all.

The Gastrea factor within her body gave her a keener sense of smell than most people, and walking down the hallway, she couldn't help but notice the strong scent of adrenaline all around. Hallways full of fear and mental strain.

Meeting up with her new homeroom teacher in her office did little to change that impression. She was Ms. Yagara, a middle-aged woman, and her laugh lines were so deep that Enju thought she might be able to stick a finger in one of them. They went even deeper whenever she so much as smiled. But despite that (as well as her unusually enormous lips), her eyes were tiny little dots, giving her a coldhearted villain look. This wasn't the type of teacher you would want to actively discuss personal issues with too much.

After some quick guidance, the homeroom bell rang and Enju was guided into the fourth-year Group Five classroom. It was time to introduce herself, and although her parental guardians often marveled at her utter lack of restraint, being planted in front of nearly forty pairs of eyes was enough to give even her pause.

"My name is Enju Aihara... I'm transferring into this school because of my parents. It's good to meet you."

She had a longer self-intro prepared but wound up toning it down for the big moment. The teacher motioned to a window-side seat in the far back row, apparently meant for her.

"Wow, transferring at a time like *this*," she heard someone whisper. It was true. Having this overlap with that whole Libra crisis was a real bummer—in several ways, selfish and otherwise.

"All right, everyone," Ms. Yagara said, demonstrating no particularly unusual interest in Enju, "I know people are all pretty nervous right now, but treat her well, all right?"

"Ms. Yagara! Hey, Ms. Yagara!" espoused a rather eager-looking boy in the front row, hand raised. "Why do we have to keep going to school if Funagasaki Elementary next door gave all the kids off?"

Nobody dared nod or show any other physical assent, but everyone in class gave him a silent agreement.

Ms. Yagara gave an ever-so-thin smile. "Well, all of *your* parents have sent you here so we can help you grow up and become fine young men and women. Besides, your parents wouldn't want you to fall behind in your studies, now would they?"

It was odd. Her tone was prim, practiced, and calm, but it was clear from her voice that she would tolerate no further dissent.

But what made everyone in class tighten their expressions was what she did afterward, taking out her class student ledger without warning.

"Now, then, I know this is sudden..."

There it was. That awkward mental strain. The smell of adrenaline Enju detected before. And it was notably, overwhelmingly in fact, coming more strongly from the girls than the boys.

Turning her eyes toward the teacher's desk, Enju saw the cold, curving smile on Ms. Yagara, an expression of pure sadistic joy.

"But I've got some special news for you all today! You probably know about Kamo over in Group Two, but all the teachers have decided to remove her from class. She's already been turned over to the IISO, which is the perfect place for Gastrea-Virus carriers like her."

Enju's body froze. Sweat poured out of her body.

"This means that there are no more carriers in our school, and I hope all of you will continue to be the best students you can possibly be for me. That is all. Oh, yes! I apologize for springing this on our new student Aihara so quickly, but we're all going on a field trip to an electrical plant in the Outer District two days from now, so I'd like everyone to form groups for me today, all right?"

Her heels clacked against the floor as she left the room.

Homeroom was over, and the students all chatted with one another during the short break that ensued. Enju, forgetting to wipe the sweat she was soaked in, kept her head down and clawed at her knees. She barely felt alive.

"Hey, I know Ms. Yagara's pretty high-strung, but don't let it bother you, okay?"

Surprised, Enju turned to her side. A girl was there, wearing a horizontal-striped skirt and a short jacket, making her look a bit like an actress from several decades ago. She must have been nervous, because she was twiddling her thumbs behind her like she was hiding something and rubbing her legs together, a self-effacing smile emerging from underneath her fluffy curls. The smile must have been what she employed to keep people from thinking she was some kind of freak, but Enju could tell she had a shy streak as well.

The girl fearfully pointed at Enju's desk.

"Aihara, is that...?"

She followed her eyes down to the laptop PCs they used for class. Enju's had a gaggle of *Tenchu Girls* stickers plastered on the back.

Drumming up all her resolve, the girl revealed what she was holding behind her back. It was a tablet, another classroom accessory, but the moment Enju's eyes fell on the back panel behind the modular screen, she lit up.

"Wh-whoa! A Tenchu Red special-color panel! You had to write in to *Girls' Dream* magazine to get that!"

Even the tablet's stylus was fully *Tenchu Girls*–themed. It was the complete package. *Who is this girl?* she thought as she sized her up again. The girl waved the tablet around in the air, snickering the snicker of someone who'd just found a fellow comrade.

"Whoa, no way! So you're commuting all the way from Magata, Enju?"

"Yeah," Enju replied as she chewed on the bread roll that came with lunch. "It takes ninety minutes to get here. I have to switch trains and everything."

The curly-haired girl, head down, was busy twirling yakisoba noodles with her fork.

"Huh. You said it was because of your parents, right? Man, that's rough. This is kind of a gifted school, too, so we get a lot of homework sometimes."

"Oh yeah?"

"Yeah. Oh, and you better watch out for Ms. Katakura, the science teacher, okay? 'Cause she totally picks kids to answer questions when they have, like, no idea."

Enju crossed her arms and nodded grimly. Every school had at least one teacher like that. The girl snickered in response.

By the time their lunch break came around, Enju and the curly-haired girl had firmly hit it off with each other. For Enju, it was reassuring—finding someone so quickly to show her around, teach her the ins and outs of school customs, and not mess around with her too much along the way. She said her name was Momoka Hieda, and already Enju and Momoka were ditching pretty much all formalities.

"Oh, hey, I live on the way to the train station. You think maybe we could walk together?"

"Sure. No problem at all."

The girl brought both hands together and smiled. "That's really great!"

Pretty cute of her, the analytical part of Enju's mind said, until she realized something else: Was *this* the kind of girl Rentaro liked?

That contrast made her think about exactly how much the parts of her mind differed.

"Hey, um, Momoka? What was with that…thing in the morning?"

The question had been filed in the back of Enju's mind for a little while now. Enju figured the time had come to ask.

"Thing? What thing?"

"Y'know, the news about that girl leaving school."

Momoka grinned, finally picking up on the topic. "Oh, yeah, that was super awkward, wasn't it? I hate it when it's like that. But a lot of people are totally in this 'expose the virus' kick here in school, and Ms. Yagara's pretty much their leader and stuff."

"So, that Kamo girl who got kicked out… Was she one of those, uh, Cursed Children or whatever they call them?"

The girl shook her head, a bit bewildered.

"I dunno."

Enju's eyes opened wide. "You don't?"

"No, I…I mean, our school's kind of different, you know? Like, I don't think it really matters if they're actually Cursed or not. If people start suspecting you, you get taken to the IISO. And even if the IISO tests you and you're not a carrier after all, like… It's kinda hard to be around here, once you're back. A lot of kids quit school after that. I heard a rumor that the school accuses kids they don't like too much of being carriers so the IISO can take them away from the place."

Aha. That explains why everyone in class—especially the girls—were so on edge back there. Rentaro told her once about how schools could be pretty closed-off, cliquish spaces at times, leading to situations you'd never expect to see anywhere else. *This must be what he was talking about.*

The girl in front of Enju flashed a broad smile, perhaps trying to cheer up her suddenly silent new friend.

"Like, as if any of us could even *be* Red-Eyes anyway, y'know?"

Enju offered a vague smile in response.

"Dahh! Okay, how about this: In episode thirteen of *Tenchu Girls*, 'Rage of the Sprawling Weeds,' you know how they fished up Carpatron from the lake? That's not, like, for real, is it?"

"I think they had one of the staff actually go over to the lake to fish there first so it'd be more realistic in story form."

"Oh. So what about 'Waiting for Godot,' episode twenty-one of the second season? Like, Tenchu Red spent the whole thirty minutes sitting in this chair waiting for Godot and talking about God and stuff. I read on the net that it was an homage to this guy named Samuel Beckett, but…"

"Yeah, I heard this overworked screenwriter had a mental breakdown and wrote that script, and the crew did it as kind of a joke. Like, make it all artsy and fancy, you know?"

"……"

"Oh, but did you know—? The final episode of the second season? Where they go into Kozuke-nosuke Kira's house to take him down? Well, it actually turns out Kira used clone tech to create seven copies of himself!"

"Whoa, whoa! Spoilers! I haven't seen that one yet!" Enju shouted, putting her hands on her ears. Momoka laughed.

The two were on their way home after what wound up being a pretty breezy curriculum for the day. It was a clear, warm summerlike day in September, the unrelenting sun tormenting their skin, but Enju's legs couldn't have felt any lighter. The sunflowers that infested the edges of school grounds were practically falling over themselves to smile at her, the cicadas summoning up their last reserves of energy to serenade the two in song.

"Boy, am I glad I went to school today."

Momoka lifted up her straw hat to take in the full sun on her face. She raised an eyebrow. "Why's that?"

"'Cause I got to meet you, Momoka."

The brim of the hat went back down as Momoka hid her face. She must not have been used to people expressing themselves so frankly like that. "Me too," she replied, her voice almost lost among the insect cries.

Then Momoka found her body being hugged tightly, as if someone had just rammed into her.

"Mom!" Momoka exclaimed, still a little bewildered at the woman who suddenly appeared. The confusion cleared up once she looked at her mother's face.

"Oh, thank heavens... Are you all right?" the woman said. She had on bronze-framed glasses, along with a lamé-finished black pantsuit, making her look like a career-track businesswoman and a helicopter parent in the making. An expensive-looking car was parked a couple steps away; she must have leaped out of it when she spotted Momoka.

"I heard there was a Red-Eyes at your school, and oh, I was just beside myself... Did she touch you or anything? She might've given you the virus."

"Oh, Mom, you don't have to worry so much! Oh, uh, lemme introduce you, Enju. This is my mother."

Momoka seemed glad to show off her mom. The woman gave a polite nod.

"Oh, thanks for making good friends with our little Momoka! I know she can be a little shy, but play nice with her, all right?"

Momoka gave her mother a playful knee. "Oh, Mommmm! Stop doing that all the time!"

"You have to wonder what those kids are thinking, though, always sneaking into school like that. Ugh, it makes me sick just thinking about it! And, you know, one of my neighbors told me that you're more likely to give birth to a Red-Eyes if you didn't want the child in the first place."

"Oh, really? 'Cause this kid in school said you could get one if you had something called an orgy."

"Momoka! Don't use *that* word! You're still too young for that."

"That's not true."

"Huh? What'd you say, Enju?"

Momoka turned an ear to her, eyes large and round. "Oh, hey, Enju, why don't you come over to my place? We could watch the second-season finale together!"

Enju lifted up her gloomy face and practically gritted her teeth, such was the effort required to force out a smile.

"Sorry, I got some stuff to do this afternoon."

Then she turned around and ran off to the station.

3

The pleasant scent of boiling soy sauce and mirin permeated the room as Rentaro flipped the contents of the frying pan with his wrist. Waiting for the food to reach the perfect level of cooking, he turned off the gas.

The doorbell chose that moment to ring. Checking his watch, he found it was already eight in the evening. Untying his apron as he opened the door, Rentaro was greeted by a tan deliveryman. "Could I get you to sign this?" he said, wielding a pen.

Rentaro picked it up and beckoned to Enju, who was watching TV inside. After a moment, she bounded over, eyes burning with curiosity.

Rentaro took the opportunity to use her head as a table to sign the receipt and return it to the deliveryman. He gave them a weird look and left.

"Ah, it's just so much more comfortable writing on your head, you know?"

Enju, apparently treating even this as a compliment, gave out a little squeal of approval. "What's in the box, though?" she asked, her curiosity returning.

Rentaro pushed her head away as she opened it. It contained two tickets. Peering at the tiny text printed on them, she realized it was a pair of free passes for the observation deck of a newly built skyscraper in nearby Magata.

They were apparently reserved for the night of the next local fireworks show, and according to the letter inside, they were from an old client—a convenience store, if Rentaro recalled correctly, having problems with some street punks hanging out there at night. The letter thanked him again, ran down everything going on since then, and invited him to enjoy some fireworks for a change of pace.

Rentaro had mixed feelings about this, but Enju was already intoning "Ohhhhhhh!" with a ticket held aloft in both arms, eyes sparkling. "We're gonna have to thank the guy who sent these to us! I can't wait for the summer festival."

"Uh, yeah—about that, Enju..." Rentaro turned back toward her. "They're probably gonna have to cancel it."

"Why?"

It was hard to watch Enju look doe-eyed at him like that, but Rentaro continued. "Things are still pretty tense with Sendai Area," he dispassionately explained. "They're sending patrol planes back and forth to intimidate each other. All it'd take is one spark to set something off, so even holding a fireworks show could be enough to push Sendai over the brink."

The neighborhood association wasn't stupid enough to fail to notice that. Chances were they'd cancel the entire festival. He expected this to crush Enju, but she was still every bit as excited as before.

"Okay, so I'll fix everything up before the festival! Then it'll be held on schedule, right?"

"Ah, there you go again with your silly nonsense..."

This problem was a little too thorny for even her to help fix, but he had to appreciate the way she could instantly pep up her spirits like that.

"Right, but let's leave that topic behind for a sec..."

"Leave it behind?"

Rentaro placed both hands on Enju's shoulders and brought his face close to hers.

"I got food ready."

Bringing out a low table, Rentaro took the bowls of rice at both stations and poured a combination of chicken, onions, and a soft-boiled egg that made its way into every nook and cranny of the dish. He felt justifiably proud of the work, and the sauce-sweetened scent of dinner wafted in the air, lovingly caressing Enju's nose.

"Eeeeeeee!"

She jumped up and down, hands still on the table, unable to restrain herself another minute.

"All right, Aihara—do you know what this dish is called?"

"*Oyako-don*, a chicken-and-egg rice bowl!" she explained, all smiles as she wiggled her rear end in the air. "Ooh, but to you and me, it's more of a *looooovers'* bowl, right?"

"That doesn't exist."

"Well, make a recipe and give it to me! Something as hot and sweaty as you and me!"

"Yeah, sure. I better think up a recipe for freeloader's rice while I'm at it, too. Something that goes cold on you in, like, five seconds."

Rentaro sat at the table, closed his eyes, solemnly brought the chopsticks to his mouth, and chewed. The sweet soy intermingled perfectly with the just-runny-enough egg. *Yes. This works. Good job, me. I wish my compatriots, the dirt-poor demon girl in the kitchen and bunny rabbit Initiator, could learn a little something from this.*

He opened an eye to find Enju rapidly packing away the bowl. *Can't be that bad for her, either,* he reasoned.

"Hey, how did school go today, Enju?"

Enju smiled back, a bit of rice on her cheek. "I made a friend!"

"Get into any problems or anything?"

Enju opened her mouth to say something but stopped and shook her head instead, smiling wryly.

"..."

Her refusal to immediately answer said enough. If Enju was opting to keep it under wraps, it didn't feel right for him to badger her.

"Enju, you can just laugh this off if I'm being too paranoid, but…don't be hesitant or anything just because I picked on you just now, all right?"

"Wh-why're you bringing *that* up?"

"I just mean, if you ever run into any problems you can't solve by yourself, don't be afraid to call on me. No matter what, I'm always gonna be at your side, okay?"

There was no telling how many times Enju might've hesitated over it in the past. For now, she just flashed an embarrassed smile and said, "Sure, all right."

Rentaro was just about to pull back and tell her to eat up while it was still hot when the doorbell rang again. *Who could that be?* he wondered as he stood up and opened the door, a little peeved.

Suddenly, something pure white flew in. He caught it in his arms, experiencing its soft texture up close and personal. Carefully, he cast his eyes downward, toward his chest. A pair of watery eyes greeted him, and his heart skipped a beat.

"You have to hide me, Mr. Satomi!"

"L-Lady Seitenshi?"

There was no mistaking the sight. It was the head of state, almost blindingly beautiful when viewed from point-blank range.

"Rentaro! No boobs!"

Rentaro froze at the uninvited commentary behind him as the Seitenshi hurriedly extracted herself.

"Wha…? What do you mean, 'hide' you?" he asked. "What're you even *doing* here—?"

The leader of Tokyo Area stretched out and stared into Rentaro's eyes.

"Would you mind if I explained inside?"

The Satomi residence, a single room around eight tatami mats large, had few perks described as desirable, apart from the low rent and the ability to befriend its many cockroaches. It was a classic dive.

The plumbing was like a never-ending comedy sketch—fix one leak, another one appeared down the pipe. The lack of soundproofing gave you a front-row seat at the radio drama of the couple next door tossing pots and pans at each other in the evenings.

Having a radiant, princesslike figure seated daintily in this hovel was a pretty unusual sight to behold. The perfumelike rose scent emanating from her did nothing to ease his mind at all. It showed, once again, just how beautiful she was.

Rentaro, hearing the Seitenshi's story with arms crossed, then lifted her head upward.

"So the guys in the palace drummed you out, and you wanna enlist me to help you get away from them?"

"Precisely."

"And you don't want to tell me why."

"Precisely."

"Could you screw around with me like this some other time?"

Rentaro's attempt at a little hard cajoling was met with an even harder stare. Her eyes indicated exactly what kind of will she had to see this through. He scratched his head in response. *Well, great. This ain't good.*

"Look, do you even realize what's going on in Tokyo Area right now?"

"All too well, I am afraid."

"And despite that, you still aren't planning on going back to the palace?"

"I am not."

"How did you escape the palace in the first place, even?"

"I cut up a curtain, fashioned it into a makeshift rope, climbed out of the window, and boarded the back of a palace food delivery truck."

Rentaro and Enju gave each other a surprised glance. Even Enju betrayed a bit of concern at this news. Was *that* all it took to elude the palace guard?

"...Uh, so how're you planning to pay my fee, anyway?"

"With this."

The Seitenshi nonchalantly removed a card from her white handbag. It was bare, case-free—she must not have been in the habit of carrying a wallet around—and judging by its silver color, Rentaro had a hunch things like credit limits and location restrictions didn't apply to this sucker.

"How'd you make it all the way over here?"

The Seitenshi gave Rentaro a funny look, apparently not understanding the point of the question.

"Well, via public transport, but…"

"Um, so you got off the train at Magata Station?"

"Yes…?"

Greeeeat. Rentaro slapped his forehead with his palm. Apparently one of Tokyo Area's most famous people didn't realize that using credit cards meant creating a virtual paper trail for yourself. And when—not if—her pursuers found out she was at Magata Station, it'd be a cinch for Rentaro's house to come up in the conversation.

His gut was telling him to turn this case down immediately. The Seitenshi didn't notice. She was too busy studying Rentaro's apartment, checking out the furniture and fixtures, novel in her eyes, before settling her eyes on the bath.

"I'm sorry, Mr. Satomi, but would I be able to use your bath?"

"The bath?"

He was about to ask why, but then he saw the mud on the hem of her outfit. One of her ankles was also swollen. Where could she have possibly been wandering before she came here? Thinking about it, he decided she must have fled the palace the day before. An entire night and day had passed until she made it here. She couldn't have been lost that whole time. Even *she* must have realized, Rentaro supposed, that making a beeline for the Satomi residence would instantly bring him under suspicion.

But in the end something about her troubles must've driven her to finally ring that doorbell. Or was that just Rentaro being overly generous with her again? It was all making her impatient, especially the sharp-eyed girl in front of her, and Rentaro couldn't help but feel a little pity for the Seitenshi.

"Ahhhh, all right. Use the bath all you want," he said, turning a finger toward the door.

"Excuse me, then," the Seitenshi responded as she stood and went inside.

Soon, in the soggy, miniscule changing area, Rentaro could hear friction between clothing and skin as the Seitenshi's dress fell to the floor. Even through the glass door, it was amazing how supple her body's silhouette was—and as Rentaro's heart quickened, the silhouette's bra dropped down as well. Surprised, he turned back to Enju. She had a fist hidden under the table, cheeks pushed out in a high state of annoyance.

"You're studying her way more closely than *me* when I undress!"

He had never "studied" her body at all—all three measurements were the same numerical value, for one—but Rentaro knew saying that would make her snap at him again. So he took the tactic of facing the opposite wall while holding his ears shut. That oughta work.

Ignoring the muffled sound of splashing water, Rentaro decided to take that moment to rewire and reorganize his thoughts. If he took this job, he'd have to take action at once. There were no handy hiding places in this apartment—even if there was, there was no way she'd escape the notice of a palace-hired professional investigator.

Then the doorbell rang a third time. *Ah, jeez, they're already on to her?*

Before he could act, though, he heard someone turning the key, unlocking the door, and turning the knob. There, standing tall, was none other than the cold-as-ice president of the Tendo Civil Security Agency. Her eyes were full of jealousy as she stormed in, her feet making sixteenth-note steps as she did.

"I smell perfume."

"Huh?"

"There's a girl here besides Enju and Tina, isn't there? It's Miori, isn't it?"

Kisara swiveled her head around, walked up to the low table, and crossed her arms.

"That," she said, "and look at you. You're sitting bolt upright."

"Y-yeah," Rentaro weakly replied to the verbal onslaught.

She narrowed her eyes into slits as she looked at him. "Look, Satomi. If you're wondering what it is I don't like about Miori, I'll tell you—it's that she knows you're my personal possession, but she still does stuff like leave her toiletry kit in your place, or a spare pair of undergarments, or she throws away my hair dryer without asking...! And you know what else? You know the cup you put your blue toothbrush in, Satomi? Well, she goes and lines it up with my red one, or marks it with her initials and stuff! I *haaaaate* that! Are you even listening?"

Rentaro had been ignoring Kisara, including her now-reddened cheeks and near-shout of a voice, because he was too busy thinking about when to come clean to her about the Seitenshi. They were both interrupted by the sound of the shower starting up. Kisara rolled her eyes over to it.

"In there, huh?"

"Hey, wait a…"

Kisara, wasting no time, stormed toward the bathroom. She was just a few inches from Rentaro's grasp when the door opened.

"Wh-whooooooaaaaaa?!"

"…Aaaaagggggghhhhh!"

Well, too late for that, then. Rentaro hung his head in shame at the two different screams emanating from his washroom. But as he did so, a light bulb went off; he slapped a fist in the palm of his hand.

That's it. The perfect hiding place for the Seitenshi.

Thirty minutes later.

The doorbell rang for a record fourth time that day. *Here we go,* Rentaro thought as he prepared to act as peeved as possible before opening up.

"You're Rentaro Satomi?"

A well-built, gray-haired man appeared, sticking a foot inside without asking. Rentaro looked down. He had a foot in position to block Rentaro from slamming the door in his face. The thick leather on his shoes indicated that he'd have no trouble doing so.

"What?"

"I'm with the palace. I can't tell you why, but I need to search your home."

"Why d'you have to do that? Go away."

"I'm afraid I can't."

The man called for someone behind him. They were invisible to Rentaro before, but suddenly a small herd of officials in white suits and palace emblems stormed into the room, passing by the increasingly flustered Rentaro. "Search everywhere," the gray-haired man said. "Under the tatami mats, over the ceilings—everything!" Enju, too busy tackling the rice bowl again, gave the men a mean look.

"Hashiba?"

Hashiba, the gray-haired man, turned toward the searcher talking to him and nodded. They were in front of the bathroom, the shower still running inside.

"There's nothing in there!"

"That's for us to decide," Hashiba warned as he pushed the door separating the bathroom from the living room. The moment he opened the door to the bath area, he found a cloud of dense fog and a short scream from the silhouette inside.

"Oh, excuse me!" Hashiba said as he tore out of the bathroom, using a handkerchief to wipe his brow. "I wish you could've told me that Miss Tendo was in there beforehand."

"I would've if you had bothered listening."

"Hashiba! I can't find her!"

Hashiba turned toward the voice. Two of his lackeys, one examining the tatami mats and the other the ceiling, gave him disappointed looks.

Rentaro opted to cross his arms like an overbearing mother.

"So, uh, what are you doing here?"

Hashiba's forehead wrinkled as he agonized over the question. Then he took a business card out of his suit and put it in Rentaro's hand.

"You can bill the palace for the damage. If Lady Seitenshi ever visits your home, I want you to use this number to contact me."

Hashiba lifted his chin in a "Let's roll" gesture as he and his men filed out, just as briskly as they had entered. Once the last of them was out of sight, Rentaro pushed down the foot pedal on his trash can and tossed Hashiba's card inside. "You can come out now," he shouted into the air as he turned around.

A few moments later, an embarrassed-looking young woman stepped out of the bathroom, arms hugging herself around her black school uniform. Behind her was the Seitenshi, trying to pretend nothing had just happened. Her hands were clasped in front of her in astonishment.

"Well done, Mr. Satomi! That was a perfect plan."

"Uh, there was nothing at all perfect about that," Kisara protested. "They all got to look at me naked!"

Not even Hashiba could have guessed that there, amidst the thick mist covering the bathroom, was the Seitenshi, body plastered against the wall in a blind spot from the entryway.

"Is that your new ninja skill?" Enju asked. "Your 'Ladies' Room Barrier of Death Jutsu'?" She made a few ninja-style moves with her hands to illustrate, evoking giggles from the Seitenshi.

"So?" Rentaro asked, scratching his head.

"So," Enju replied, "I assume that means we're taking her request."

"Actually, I do have one more request. The *real* one I have to make, if anything."

"Ah, crap, do you ever bring me any good news?"

The Seitenshi smiled thinly at Rentaro's complaint as she crossed her arms.

"President Tendo…Mr. Satomi…I'd like you to bring back two items for me. One is called Solomon's Ring, and the other is the Scorpion's Neck."

4

The crystalline object the Seitenshi brought with her was a shade of royal blue, compact enough that an uninformed observer would have assumed it was a sapphire jewel. She instructed Rentaro to turn down the lights; when he did, the crystal shone a deep blue, and suddenly a giant holographic model appeared in the center of the room. The light displayed a building that resembled a factory.

"The incident took place five days ago at a laboratory in Russia."

The model, reacting to her voice, expanded out and populated with a set of photographs. There was a machine room with parts lying all over the place, traces of blood and tape outlines on the floor. Probably taken by the local police, Rentaro assumed. The room had been fairly well ransacked. It was clear the criminals were looking for something. The tape and the bloodstains were the only things the victims had left for the world.

Rentaro, chopsticks in hand, frowned as he shifted his gaze between his rice bowl and the images projected in front of him. It wasn't exactly his choice of dinner entertainment.

"Somebody broke into this lab and made off with some top-secret research material."

"The 'items' you were talking about earlier?" Enju asked quizzically.

The Seitenshi courteously nodded. "One of them, yes. The work was being conducted under the code name Solomon's Ring. I believe it's involved with the current case we're facing here, in some way or another."

"Solomon's Ring?" Kisara interjected. "The ring from the legend of King Solomon that lets him talk to animals and stuff?"

Rentaro gave her a look of admiration. She pouted in response. "Everyone should know *that* much."

"So," Rentaro said, turning back to the Seitenshi, "is that ring what you want us to get back for you?"

"It's just a code name, as I mentioned before. In reality, it is a translation device—one the Russian government is developing to communicate with Gastrea."

"Wha—?!"

Rentaro wasn't the only one taken aback. He exchanged glances with Kisara and Enju, both rendered statuelike.

"They can do that...?"

The Seitenshi shook her head. "Just in a very limited, fractional manner. It sounds like they've been able to communicate simple ideas to the Gastrea, although they don't know what all the screams and cries in response mean."

"So, what did these guys break into the lab for?"

"I'll admit that I did not pay particular attention to the incident when I first heard about it. Not until Libra appeared."

"Wait..."

The Seitenshi's narrowed eyes shone in the dimness. "At almost the same time, someone broke into a research lab in Tokyo Area and massacred the researchers inside. Between the location and their modus operandi, it's almost certainly the same group. And while they were there..."

"...They took that 'Scorpion's Neck' thing?"

The moment the name came up, Rentaro had already resigned himself somewhat to his fate. He recalled his battle with the Zodiac Gastrea Scorpion, the Stage Five that appeared during Kagetane Hiruko's assault on the city, one of the strongest of all Gastrea, and the one that made Rentaro's current path in life all but unavoidable. It was not a name he was expecting to ever hear again.

"Precisely. We had recovered the body of Scorpion after you two—the Rentaro Satomi/Enju Aihara pair—destroyed it, and we were having them research it in secret."

"Would asking why be a stupid question?"

"Gastrea cadavers, particularly Zodiac-class ones, are extremely difficult to come by. There are hundreds of research groups that would give their right arm for even a few tissue samples."

"So, what do these two break-ins have to do with Libra?" Kisara couldn't help but ask.

"Ever since eleven Zodiac Gastrea appeared at the same time worldwide ten years ago, we've theorized that Stage Five–level creatures can 'speak' to one another through their cries. And when they took Scorpion's Neck—or, to be exact, the vocal cords we extracted from Scorpion—and gave them an electrical stimulus while steeped in a cellular activator, it generated a mixture of electrical and sonic waves. It just sounds like information-free noise to us, so it's been a mystery to wave-analysis researchers across the world."

"And the Solomon's Ring translator might be the key to solving that riddle?"

"Like I said," the Seitenshi continued instead of answering Kisara's question, "the Ring is still under development. There's almost no actual communication that can be made with what few species they've had any success with, but apparently Libra is the sole exception."

Rentaro rubbed his chin with a finger, pondering this. "Hang on a sec," he said. "If Libra occupied Mount Nasu immediately after those two robberies, are you saying it's in that Varanium mine and building up its stock of viruses because someone's directing it to?"

"...I'm saying it is possible. We're talking two different laboratories that were targeted at once."

"So why isn't the palace trying to do anything about that? This is serious!"

"I'm sad to say that everything you've heard so far is little more than conjecture. If we explained this to the other Areas without any evidence, they might just see it as us trying to make excuses. It's not a lie, after all, that the Inheritance of the Seven Stars has the power to attract Gastrea. It's hard to blame Prime Minister Ino for concluding that Tokyo Area is the culprit."

She tapped a finger rapidly on her still-crossed arms.

"So this whole disaster's thanks to your government covering every-thing up, isn't it?" Rentaro fired back. "I mean, if it looks like a duck and it quacks like a duck...you know?"

"I am willing to take the criticism for that, yes. We have secrets, and these secrets open us up to questioning. But you would have known that, Mr. Satomi, after your military training under the Tendo family. Prime Minister Kaihoko would have, too, as would President Saitake. Even if we disclosed the Inheritance to the public, do you believe they would use that strictly for peaceful purposes?"

"...Who would even do something this crazy, anyway?"

"Both groups used small arms for their attacks. Judging by that and their methods, they were both professional outfits. Surveillance foot-age showed that one of their members is currently wanted by inter-national authorities for terrorist activity."

The Seitenshi rotated the laboratory floor plan in the air, tapping on a corner to expand it. The video screen showed a clear overhead view from a distant height as a man in a tactical vest pointed a rifle toward the camera view. The ski mask on his face prevented any pos-itive identification.

"So we don't know anything about them?"

"Not necessarily." She tapped away at a holographic keyboard, trimming down the image to focus on the masked attacker's eyes. An analysis of his irises flashed on-screen, comparing the results with an international terror database and bringing up a photograph of a white male, accompanied by a detailed history of his life.

"This is Marc Meyerhold. A native of Belarus who spent seven years with Russian Spetsnaz special forces. Voice scans also picked up two or so other Belarusians with criminal histories in their homeland."

"Belarus? But didn't Belarus...?"

The Seitenshi gave an approving nod. "Right. The Greater Minsk Area, which served as the capital of Belarus, was flattened by none other than Libra itself. That struck my curiosity, so I looked over some materials from the final days of Greater Minsk. It...wasn't pretty."

She closed her eyes for a moment, lost in melancholy, then turned back to Rentaro.

"There's something else I want to tell you, Mr. Satomi. These terrorists used to work under Andrei Litvintsev."

This chilled Rentaro to his core. "Andrei Litvintsev?"

He knew the name. It was one he couldn't forget, no matter how
hard he tried.

"Who's that?" asked a confused Enju.

Rentaro turned to her. "You remember half a year ago? When that
dude down the street was bitching at us about this weirdo going in and
out of his neighbor's house? That guy."

Enju slapped a fist against her palm. "Ohhh! The illegal immigrant?"

Kisara sighed. "A lot more than that. It turned out to be the big-
gest spy-exposure case in Japan since Richard Sorge back in 1941. The
newspapers were going nuts over it."

Rentaro turned his head back to his leader. "Where is he right now?"

"He's serving a life sentence in Mega-Float Prison. We believe he
was heavily involved with the lab attacks, so we've been negotiating
with him for info in exchange for reducing his sentence, but…"

"…But he's staying mum?"

"It might be worse than that, even…particularly for you, Mr.
Satomi."

"What do you mean?"

The Seitenshi suddenly found it difficult to find the right words.
Rentaro looked on silently.

"Litvintsev…has asked you to mediate over the negotiations, Mr.
Satomi."

Waves of discomfort flowed over Rentaro's mind. He lowered his
brows. "Me? Why me?"

"We don't know. All we know is that Litvintsev says he's willing to
negotiate if we send you over."

Rentaro looked aside and prodded his chin to mull this over. "So
these two labs in Russia and Tokyo Area were attacked, and you
think there's a pretty good chance Litvintsev and his people are using
what they stole from them to control Libra, right? What are their
motives for that?"

"We don't know that, either. The palace hasn't received any demands
or claims of responsibility from anyone. But right now, I think figuring

this out is less important than taking action, and quickly. Time's ticking away as we speak. Counting today, we have three days to eliminate the threat of Libra and prevent an all-out war between Tokyo and Sendai Area. Before then, I want you to travel to Mega-Float Prison, meet with Litvintsev, and find out where his friends are hiding."

The city of Magata at night was windless and quiet. Not even a single insect or bird cry could be heard. The moon shone at an acute angle as the occasional car roared down the side street.

"I absolutely reeeee-*fuse* to accept this!"

The hapless Rentaro extended a weak hand to Kisara, storming down the sidewalk with shoulders whisking back and forth.

"Well, what do you want me to do? My place is about the only safe spot she's got right now."

Kisara suddenly stopped, making Rentaro run into her nose-first. He stumbled a bit in surprise as she turned around, hands on her hips.

"That's not the issue, you idiot! I'm saying that a woman like Lady Seitenshi can*not* sleep under the same roof as a guy!"

Rentaro looked up at the heavens for divine assistance.

They'd agreed to respond to the Seitenshi's request at a later time before moving the topic of conversation to where she would spend the night. Rentaro had suggested his room, which had immediately incensed Kisara. Considering Rentaro's apartment was the only place she was safe from palace searchers, there was really no choice. But for some reason, Kisara found that difficult to accept. All evening, it had been nothing but "No, no, *no!*" from her.

Rentaro sighed. "You really don't trust me that much?"

"How could I ever trust you?" She pouted, blushing, her voice low. "Besides, you attacked *me* once."

Sweat shot out of Rentaro's body as the surface temperature on his face skyrocketed.

"No, that...that was, um..."

His mind returned to the events of a month ago while his mouth continued to fumble for an excuse. He had been framed for the murder of his old acquaintance Kihachi Suibara, which indirectly led him to discover and break the door open on the Black Swan Project and crush Atsuro Hitsuma's diabolical plans. It wasn't long after that when subsequent events had led Rentaro to kiss Kisara, and right after that—

"Listen, uh…back then, Kisara, why did you—?"

"…Ohhh!" She clapped her hands as she turned her head back up. "R-right! Now I remember. I was gonna pick up some groceries during the big sale they're having. Tina's probably hungry and stuff, so I'll let you go for now, Satomi. See you!"

"Whoa, hey—"

There was no time to say anything as Kisara ran off and gradually faded into the cityscape. He tried to give chase for a while, only to wind up completely alone on the little landing in front of the entrance to Magata Park. Looking at the clock lit up among the playground equipment, he realized it was half an hour past midnight. If there were any nearby grocery stores open at that time of night, Rentaro wasn't aware of them.

"What the hell was *that* about…?"

"Hey, I'm back," a still-troubled Rentaro said as he discarded the shoes he had hurriedly put on a few minutes prior. The first thing he saw was the uncommon sight of Enju and the Seitenshi sitting next to each other, the latter in a prim and proper kneel, while the former tried to mimic her in the most ladylike manner possible. They were both focused on the TV.

It was some sort of live broadcast from the palace, which was lit up and surrounded by crowds of people. A reporter was in the midst, gripping a microphone tightly with both hands as she summoned her most authoritative voice.

"One night after the palace held an emergency press conference, the Zodiac Gastrea Libra remains curled up in the Mount Nasu area. It has yet to move an inch."

The image shifted to some previously shot aerial footage of the mountain area.

"Libra…"

Its long, thin body was curled into a ball, its fearsome, reptilelike visage resembling a snake's—or maybe even a dragon's. The viral sacs

weren't visible from this vantage point, but there was no doubt they were still expanding, inflating, waiting for just the right moment to unleash their payload.

"*Tensions remain high between Tokyo Area and Sendai Area, as Tokyo responds to the shutdown of their embassy in Sendai with a shutdown of Sendai's. Prime Minister Ino doubled down earlier on his accusation that Libra was summoned by the Seitenshi administration, and Sendai aircraft are still conducting patrols around Libra and nearby Tokyo Area. Palace officials have yet to release a formal comment about this, but reports indicate that intensive negotiations are taking place beneath the surface at Lady Seitenshi's command.*"

The Seitenshi scowled.

"Hey, uh, you think it's about time you head home?"

"Mr. Satomi..."

She must have just noticed Rentaro then, her fetching but gloom-filled visage turning toward him as she shook her head.

"I will not."

Enju, unable to stay ladylike any longer, shot to her feet.

"This is so boring, Rentaro. All the channels are showing this stupid live coverage. They preempted the *Tenchu Girls* special!"

"Hey, even magical-girl fighters need a break now and then." Rentaro handed the complaining girl some new underwear, prodding her into the bathroom to take her evening bath. He was glad to get some peace and quiet—or, at least, he was until Enju stuck her head out the door and said "No peeking!" with a cheesy grin.

"Who's gonna peek at *you*?"

Picking up on some giggling next to him, Rentaro turned to the Seitenshi, who had a hand to her mouth.

"Ah, children are so honest, aren't they?"

"Nah. Enju probably didn't even understand half of what we were talking about anyway."

"Well, does anyone though, really? I'm half in doubt about it myself."

Their conversation faded just as a new advertisement came on, an upbeat melody accompanying a burst of light that illuminated both their faces as it ran across the screen.

"May I ask you for a response to my request pretty soon? That's what you were discussing with President Tendo, no?"

"Oh. Yeah. That."

He had tried to discuss it, at least, but Kisara ran off before he could. It was all still up in the air. Rentaro focused on the TV instead. The ad was over, and now the news was showing a photo of Tokyo Area's Sendai ambassador and his family, still being held in his embassy by the local authorities.

"We'll take it. I'll tell my boss about it later."

"Um, are you sure Ms. Tendo doesn't need to be informed?"

"Yeah, I'm sure. If I tell her I'm gonna do something, she never opposes me. As long as I'm strong enough with it, I mean."

Almost immediately, Rentaro began to doubt himself. Did he take the job in order to stop some unknown pain and sadness coming in the world's future? Or was it just to take a dig at the indecisive Kisara? He shook his head, realizing he was turning into someone he didn't like very much, and decided to stop thinking. The reasonable side of his mind refused to advance this line of thought any further.

The smoke that wisped up from the piggy bank–shaped mosquito-repellent holder was buffeted by the fan that whizzed back and forth in the darkness, leaving a sharp chemical odor as it vaporized into the air.

Sleep was apparently going to be something rather distant tonight, since Rentaro's consciousness was operating at full capacity. Putting both hands behind his head, he found himself tracing the grains on the grimy wooden ceiling with his eyes. There was a rustling, followed by someone grunting a little in his ear. He felt breath on his neck, tickling him enough that he turned to his side.

There was the sleeping face of Enju, almost close enough to touch. And across from Enju's futon was the Seitenshi, arms crossed in front of her, the picture of infallible tranquility as her chest rhythmically rose and fell. She was wearing a pink nightgown—part of the sleepover kit Miori brought with her long ago—but that did nothing to stain the sheer beauty and elegance that emanated from her face.

Rentaro got up to relieve himself, then tiptoed to the refrigerator and polished off a half-consumed sports drink. The cold liquid flowed down to his warm stomach. He turned toward the nearby window. It was a bright night, the moonlight coming down on his surroundings at an angle.

Suddenly he noticed, among the choir of summer insects gathered outside his door, another voice, almost hidden. He turned toward it and swallowed nervously. It was the Seitenshi, her back turned—and she was sobbing, her shoulders shaking.

"Are you all right?" he asked, kneeling down to put a hand on one shoulder. She instantly spun around. Her eyes, practically drained of tears, sparkled as they reflected the moonlight. It made Rentaro freeze for a moment as the insects rattled their wings against one another, droning the night away.

Then his brain went back to a question he had been dwelling on all day: Why did the Seitenshi flee the palace in the first place? He had been lightly prodding her about that since she'd arrived. It was possible, he reasoned, that she was here on a covert basis...that perhaps Kikunojo was against leaving the negotiations with Litvintsev in Rentaro's hands.

But was that really it? The Seitenshi wasn't just some bureaucrat; she was the head of a nation, its commander-in-chief, and the chain of command made it clear that there was no one in Tokyo Area allowed to order her around. She had every right to turn down Kikunojo's advice and call on the services of the Tendo Civil Security Agency anytime she wanted.

So why, then?

The Seitenshi, still shaking, grabbed at the sleeve of Rentaro's pajamas, head down.

"Every day, lately, I've been putting my hand on my Bible and asking it what I should do. But no matter how hard I try...all I am for this city is window dressing." The despair was clear in her voice. "As far as our citizens are concerned...Kikunojo is more than enough for them. I... They don't need me...!"

"Lady Seitenshi..."

"It pains me. I want to live my life under the firm belief that there is a good, and virtuous, side to everyone. But everyone around me is swept up by hatred instead. Mr. Satomi, what...? What should I...?!"

Leave it to me; Don't worry; It'll all be okay—assorted phrases crossed Rentaro's mind, but none had the strength to reach his lips.

Instead, he placed his palms over her clenched fists and held them, silently.

BLACK BULLET 7 CHAPTER 02

THE BULLET THAT CHANGED THE WORLD

The winds of war may have been blowing across Tokyo Area, but the weather determinedly refused to play the part. It was gloriously sunny, and Rentaro was constantly surrounded by the symphony of late-summer insects as he walked on.

After seeing Enju off to class and informing Magata High School that he wouldn't be in today, he wiped the sweat off his brow and immediately took the bus to Magata University Hospital. The receptionist waved him through, and in another moment, he was headed toward Sumire's laboratory, going down a stairway so steep that it seemed to descend into an abyss. There was one issue he wanted to get straight with himself before he sat down with Litvintsev.

"Doctor, are you—?"

Before he could finish, there was a bang and Rentaro noticed something whizzing through the air toward him.

"Aghh...?!"

He promptly blocked his face. Then he felt something light and fluffy cover his head. He slowly opened his eyes and removed the aluminum casing and shredded paper that had been launched, crumpling it up. In the midst of this, the university's living ghost story had appeared in front of him, wearing Groucho glasses and a conical party hat. Just like that, she tossed the cracker she'd deployed at Rentaro's face into the garbage.

"Congratulations, Satomi!"

She pulled a string to her side, opening up a large ball strapped to the ceiling. From it unfurled a banner that read RENTARO SATOMI: CONDOLENCES FOR GETTING DUMPED BY KISARA.

Rentaro could feel himself getting dizzy.

"...Doctor, come on. You weren't waiting to ambush me just so you could do *this*, were you?"

"'Do unto others what annoys them the most.' The Muroto family motto."

The woman in the lab coat removed the glasses, the grin behind the fake mustache now glaringly obvious.

"Why did your parents marry each other, Doctor?"

"A mystery that time may never unravel, my friend. Now, then—" Sumire sat down on a chair, about to die of sheer joy. "You got dumped?"

"I didn't get dumped, Doctor."

"Well, give me some details, then. I only got the CliffsNotes version over the phone. Don't be so afraid to ask for help, man. Dr. Muroto, love adviser, at your service!"

She winked, gave the peace sign, and stuck out her tongue. It didn't exactly befit her age. Rentaro was struck dumb.

"You've got enough love experience to advise people, Doctor?"

"Nooooo! The only loves I've had in life were all cold and rotting by the time they got carted in here. Even the one man I *did* love wound up dead at the end of it. So, corpses, mostly. Basically, if they're breathing, they can go screw themselves, as far as I'm concerned."

"Does that count for me, too?"

"Uh, yeah? Did you think I had a thing going for you, you piece of garbage? Pfft!"

"Whoa! Don't spit on me, man!"

Something about the way Sumire used the word *dumped* made him grit his teeth. Maybe it was because he couldn't deny it out of hand. From an impartial perspective, it might look that way.

"...What's the point in asking you for advice, anyway?" Rentaro asked, his heart still reeling.

Sumire shrugged. "Well, is there anything I can help you with?"

"..."

Rentaro brooded to himself as he sat on a stool, staring at the floor. Could he really be honest with Sumire? He ran a finger along his lips. The chill it evoked helped him recall past events with more clarity.

Stopping the Black Swan Project helped mend their frayed relationship beyond all expectation...and it led Rentaro to take just one step forward to close the distance. But what happened next went completely beyond his expectations: Kisara turned completely ashen, started to shake, and, hugging her own body, pushed Rentaro away and ran off.

He thought it was some error on his part at first, but looking back through his memories, that really didn't seem to be the case. No matter how much he dwelled on it, though, he couldn't figure it out. Even now, he had no idea why she acted like that. She dodged the question whenever he tried to ask her, leaving his heart feeling like it was hanging in midair.

"I don't think this is just a matter of a woman's whimsy or anything," Sumire said, eyes now serious as she propped her elbow on the table.

"...You aren't gonna pick on me? Like, 'You went too fast and started rubbing her assets,' or anything?"

"Well, if that's what you want, then sure. But that's just gonna depress you even more, wouldn't it? I like to strike a balance, you know? Don't leave 'em dead, but don't let 'em live. It wouldn't be any fun unless you roused yourself back into shape and went at her again, after all."

She phrased it jokingly, but Rentaro's heart still found itself lightened. He could feel a thin strand of sympathy between the words. He thanked her internally.

"I think," he said, "Kisara feels kind of guilty at the idea that she can find happiness in her life."

"Why?" Sumire grudgingly asked, almost rising off her chair. "Just chill out. You know full well that Kisara got her groove back because she's using her desire to avenge her parents as an emotional support. It's been a long time, but I had a chance to look at her medical records back during my practicing days. It was stuff like her insulin dosages, the interviews they conducted when she underwent counseling after her parents were killed, that kind of thing. One thing I remember seeing in there is that she said whenever she feels happiness, it triggers feelings for her dead parents. Apparently she had visions of them every now and then. They'd be standing there like ghosts, and they'd admonish her for leaving them behind. They begged her for revenge."

"No way..."

It was like the ghostly king from *Hamlet*. But unlike that apparition, Rentaro could hardly believe that Kisara's parents, Osamu and Yomiko, would choose those words for their daughter.

"Anyway, I checked it again a while later, and all that material had been struck from her records. The doctor wrote at the end of it that she had gotten over her depression and was ready to tackle life on her own. It was a little too neat and pretty for my tastes. You saw how she got revenge against someone just a bit ago, right? It wouldn't be weird at all if she's letting those visions bother her again."

"..."

Even if it were true, that explanation would never please Rentaro's heart. He scratched his head to calm down.

"Are you sure you should be giving other people's medical information to me, Doctor?"

Sumire shrugged. "Don't go asking a no-good doctor like me for morals, please."

"Guess I owe you one."

"Oh, no need to repay the favor. If I started expecting you to repay them at this point, I'd have to get reincarnated before you finally made up the difference. Still, though..." Sumire paused to stretch herself out, arms wide. "We've got two Areas ready to declare war on each other, and here you are worrying your little head about love, huh? Are your danger sensors screwed up or something?"

"And what do you think about a war, Doctor?"

"I think it's a total waste of time. What's the point of killing one another? We're all gonna die anyway." She gave a defiant grin. "None of us can escape it. Sooner or later, it dawns on us all that there's no point trying to resist death."

"You're the same as always, huh?"

Sumire raised her arms up dramatically. "I am simply here to offer praise unto death. Death, you see, is death. People like you, trying to find some deeper emotion or meaning to it—that's what I don't understand."

Rentaro got up off his stool.

"There's something about this situation I wanted to ask you about, Doctor. Two labs in Russia and Japan were attacked. Someone broke into them and stole two items: Solomon's Ring and the Scorpion's Neck."

Sumire's eyes twinkled. "Go on."

He did, telling her everything the Seitenshi said yesterday, having received permission from her to ask Sumire for advice.

"Hmm...Solomon's Ring, huh? Pretty fancy name for a dumb little translation device."

Sumire stared blankly into space.

"'Wise King Solomon talked about animals and birds, reptiles and fish.' The First Book of Kings from the Old Testament. I think the story about putting on Solomon's Ring to understand animals came from a mistranslation in another edition or something."

"Do you know anything about it?"

"No," she said, her face troubled. "I focused my studies on mechanized soldiers that could fend off Gastrea. I never looked at ways we could tame them or anything. It's a pretty novel approach, I think, but judging by how incomplete it is, I'm guessing they probably hit a wall somewhere."

"If you combine that with Scorpion's vocal cords, though, I think you might be able to give orders to Libra, at least. We can't just ignore those things."

"A fair enough thing to keep in mind, true. I'm afraid there's not much help I can give when it comes to Russian translation devices. But if this stare down between Tokyo and Sendai keeps going, I have a pretty good hunch how it'll turn out."

"Full-on war, right?"

"No, even worse," Sumire barked, like a teacher admonishing a wayward student. "I'm talking worldwide nuclear warfare. World War III."

Rentaro stared at Sumire, forgetting to breathe for a moment. "Wh-whoa, Doctor," he managed to spit out. "Haven't you been watching the news?" He smiled, trying to classify Sumire's response as a joke. But there was no humor in her stone-cold face.

"Reality, Satomi, is a nightmare that always unfolds one step ahead of where you expect it to. Turn on the TV."

He grabbed the remote thrown at him, pointed it at the musty old television in one corner, and turned it on. It just barely sputtered into action, the image slowly coming into focus.

It showed a number of ships pushing their way through the waves—cruisers, destroyers, supply boats, all accompanying a much larger battleship piercing its way through the wind. A nuclear carrier, it looked like. No Area in Japan as of 2031 had one in its possession—they simply cost too much to build and maintain. He assumed this was some drama at first, but a familiar news network logo in the corner convinced him otherwise.

The text below told the story. US Activates Naval Fleet: Accuses Tokyo Area of Violating Bio-weapon Treaty. And before Rentaro could recover, the screen switched again, this time showing another fleet—this one apparently from Russia.

"*This is the latest footage of the American and Russian fleets as they make their way toward Tokyo Area waters,*" a harried-looking commentator said as the studio cameras focused on him. He looked at his wits' end, and that was the final confirmation Rentaro needed. This was no large-scale practical joke after all.

"What the hell?" he said, turning around. "'Bio-weapon treaty'...?"

He found Sumire glumly staring at the screen. "Things took a turn for the worse while you were on your way here. That's an international biological weapons treaty they're talking about. That's what they're probably interpreting the Inheritance of the Seven Stars to be, since it supposedly controls Stage Fives and stuff. The US claims we're violating that treaty. They're demanding inspections in all Areas, including the palace in Tokyo Area. I'm sure we'll refuse, but..."

"Why're foreign nations getting involved? It's just between the two Areas."

Sumire gave Rentaro a commiserative look. "On the surface, it's because Tokyo Area asked its allies for help. Russia, the UK, France—they've got priority Varanium-supply relationships with those countries. Why do they ask for help? Because Sendai's asked for help from its own allies in the US, Australia, and China, of course. The real reason for this, though, is a little different."

"What do you mean?"

"Any type of natural resource dug up from the ground is inevitably distributed across planet Earth in an uneven fashion. Africa's got gold and diamonds; the Middle East has oil; that sort of thing. And in the case of Varanium, the top nation just happens to be Japan. Tokyo Area alone produces thirty-one percent of the world's Varanium supply. Sendai Area has sixteen percent. If Sendai fell apart and Tokyo managed to expand its territory—and, with that, their mining rights—that's almost half the Varanium in the world, right in their hands. And it's the same deal vice versa. If Sendai decides to open fire on Tokyo before Libra releases its viral sacs—let me remind you, an exhausted Tokyo after fending off both Scorpion and Aldebaran—then *bam*, they've got an oligopoly on forty-seven percent of the world supply. And do you know what that would mean?"

"No...?" Rentaro replied, voice clearly nervous.

"We all need Varanium to survive. It's used to build our Monoliths, not to mention our weapons and ammo. If a single nation controlled half the world's supply, it could basically name its price for the stuff."

Rentaro made a startled gasp.

"They see what's going on with the other nations, too. For example, let's say that Tokyo Area had to rely on imports for one hundred percent of its food. If the other Areas decided to ban exports to Tokyo, we'd pretty much have to be their lapdogs. Even if they set the prices sky-high, we'd still have to buy it, right? So depending on how this little skirmish between two Far East city-states works out, one of us might wind up controlling the very fates of the rest of the world. That's something other nations would like to avoid at all costs. It sounds like the US and Russia have their fingers on the nuclear buttons right now, but the fact that grown-ups like that are getting involved with this playground squabble has everything to do with Tokyo's untapped resources. It's a curse, in a way."

"But isn't there a noninterference treaty between the Areas or anything?"

"Not really. The five Areas of Japan are treated as independent nations, after all."

Rentaro quickly searched his head for something to counter with. It was proving to be a struggle.

"Well... Well, so won't the UN do anything? That's their job, isn't it, to step in between conflicts like this?"

Sumire shrugged, like she'd known this was coming. "The UN's been pretty much dysfunctional ever since the Gastrea came along. And even if they weren't, what could they do? It's not like they could stop the Cold War from happening. That's what the twentieth century should've taught us all—once things get too big, it's beyond anyone's ability to stop it."

The TV now showed a set of pundits, each wailing in their own creative way about Japan's current uncertain future.

"Satomi," Sumire said, voice more gentle now, "you've probably read about World War I in your history book, haven't you? Do you know why that war happened in the first place?"

Rentaro shook his head, lost.

"On June 28, 1914, a young Serbian man involved in a clandestine terror organization just happened to come across a car carrying an Austrian archduke that had taken a wrong turn in Sarajevo. He took the chance to shoot the guy down, and the fallout made the already-unsteady relationships between the European nations, Turkey, and Russia even worse. That led to World War I, and well over ten million people died because of it. And look at the Battle of Lexington. That was fought outside of Boston on April 19, 1775. The US colonies didn't have the nerve to stage a full revolution against Britain yet, and when the American commander saw British troops advancing, he was within seconds of giving the retreat order. But then someone or other fired a shot, and all hell broke loose. The proverbial shot heard 'round the world—nobody knows who shot it, but there you go. The bullet from the Serbian, the bullet in Lexington—both of those trigger pulls changed the world."

"…What are you getting at?"

"I'm saying, once things go all the way to the very edge, all it takes is a single bullet to start a war. And once it starts, it won't stop until an astonishing number of people are dead. Right now, Tokyo Area and Sendai Area are both fanning the flames—closing their embassies and their airports. If that's not playing it on the brink, I don't know what is. All it'd take is one more bullet. It's a lot more serious than you could ever imagine."

Sumire placed both elbows on the desk and put her chin on her crossed arms.

"Satomi, you need to start negotiating with Andrei Litvintsev as soon as possible. You're the only one left with any control over this. Don't let anyone fire another bullet that changes the world."

Then she grinned, as if recalling a joke.

"The fate of the world might be resting on your shoulders right now."

2

During the Gastrea War ten years ago, when Tokyo put up the final temporary Monolith and shut the Gastrea out of the city for good, the people's hearts were filled not with relief from returning to safety but with a mix of boundless despondency and a sneaking suspicion that it wasn't really over.

When Prime Minister Zama, head of state at the time, announced on TV, radio, and the Internet that the war was over, most people greeted the news with warm tears, even if they didn't know where their reaction was coming from. The tears symbolized sadness for the people who were killed, chagrin at losing the war, and a deep melancholy, a self-reckoning over what they had just done with their lives.

Soon after, the last prime minister to rule over a united Japan lost his standing in the political world when, fearing for a Japan whose population was ten percent of what it was before, he placed intense pressure on the medical world to institute a blanket ban on abortion. This ban ultimately led to an explosive growth of what would later become known as the Cursed Children. The lack of access to birth control also led to an increase in unwanted children, causing a rash of abandonment and abuse—and indirectly leading to the urban legend that illegitimate children were more likely to be Cursed.

Zama, ironically enough, met his demise in 2029 on the way to the hospital after one of the Cursed Children his policies allowed to be born snapped his neck in two. His rule was followed by the first Seitenshi, who worked to merge the city of Tokyo with the scattered prefectures that surrounded it to create the forty-three districts of Tokyo Area.

After the end of the war, the Area was faced with a mountain of tasks—repairing broken infrastructure, solving the Area's endemic power shortages, procuring a reliable food supply, and securing more territory for the large population crammed into this relatively small space. That led to the construction of the so-called Mega-Float, an artificial island off Tokyo Bay.

Construction on the bay had been frequent and vigorous before, but after the war, the shore was so densely packed that the buildings were eating into the bay itself, literally changing the map.

And now Rentaro stood in front of one.

The heavy shadow of a bird crossed the ground. Rentaro looked up, exposing his face to the torturous sun. He raised a hand to his forehead as the cries of some distant shorebird hit his eardrums. Probably a flock of seagulls, he figured, lazily working their way along the seaside. They were called *umineko* in Japanese, literally *sea cat*, because of their distinctive cry—a cry that Rentaro always thought sounded more like an infant than anything.

Seagulls, he didn't mind so much. Especially compared to the herring gulls that shared this shore with them. They were stupid birds. Stealing chicks from other nests, ripping them apart and feeding them to their own, or sometimes taking them for their own babies and raising them instead. Ugh.

Rentaro would've wanted to continue exploring the natural knowledge he had encased in his brain for a while longer, but he stopped himself and eyed the ominous-looking entrance before him. This was part of the rush of sloppily built construction the Area saw after the war; despite being less than a decade old, the white outer walls already sported cracks and falling plaster. There was a rustic feel to it, like an old seaside sanatorium, coupled with an inscrutable sense of pure evil.

This was Tokyo Area's District 32 Offshore Criminal Detention Center.

Among the chaos people had to endure in the postwar years was a short but intense period of hyperinflation, with a box of cornflakes almost reaching 100,000 yen for a time. But that was a common occurrence in history—things like 1,000-yen and 10,000-yen bills were just pieces of paper, after all; they only held value because of the good name and trust people held in the Japanese government. The Gastrea War cost these bills their liquidity, and once the Tokyo Stock Exchange shut down, people's trust in their currency went right with it.

In the ensuing months, it wasn't unusual to see entrepreneurs with money to burn a few days ago suddenly being forced to poke around garbage cans for food. There was, naturally, an accompanying increase in crime.

Most cases involved people with no other choice but to break the law—but there were light and dark sides to every person. People who lost their sense of guilt after committing one crime and getting away with it; people whose crimes escalated thanks to the adrenaline thrill they got... This offshore prison was built for people like that, people who took a step over that most final of lines.

Looking back the way he'd come, Rentaro eyed the impossibly long wharf. The only thing visible on it was a solitary gate and guard booth. Despite being considered part of the Outer Districts, this bay-side locale was free of rubble; it had been fully revitalized, in fact, the crescent-shaped bay around it now a beachfront park. It was an urban oasis of sorts, lined with lovers walking shoulder to shoulder, mothers pushing strollers, and activity centers for the elderly. Then there was this prison. It was cut off, separate.

Rentaro gave his name and civsec license to the man at the front desk. He looked rather surprised when Rentaro asked for an urgent meeting with Litvintsev. He left for a moment, then brought back an older guard who said, "Come with me." Rentaro followed, hands balled into fists as he prepared to face this most final of confrontations.

"Ah, you civsecs come pretty young these days... You're the guy who arrested Litvintsev?"

It wasn't until they passed the second locked door that the guard leading him had finally opened his mouth.

"Well, by sheer coincidence...but yeah."

"I dunno if you know, but you won't find any normal prisoners in here. These are all people who were too much for our other facilities to handle."

"Yeah, looks like it," Rentaro said as he looked around. There wasn't a single light on. It felt empty, with only the sounds of their footsteps filling the space. Small, barred windows dotted the walls at regular intervals, and light flowed diagonally down. It smelled like the sea, and the sound of seagulls in the air was incessant—and, once Rentaro looked hard enough, he spotted the lenses of surveillance cameras on all four corners of the ceiling. There were lines of holes in the floor, which he assumed contained metal bars that shot up in case something happened.

He was also surprised to find some girls among the security staff. One was seated on a chair, with one leg over the other, as she tapped her foot nervously. There was a spade symbol painted below her right eye, like she was part of some underground club scene; it was clear she was trying to project a bad-girl image.

"Wow, you've got Initiators on payroll here?"

"Transfers from the IISO, yes. Not sure we need them, though. It's kind of going overboard with the security."

Rentaro turned his head toward a particular bit of darkness that seemed to waver for just a moment. A pair of sharply lit eyes followed his movements silently from a darkened cell. He didn't know what the guy was in for, nor did he care, but it was clear he was one of the prisoners. The way he remained perfectly silent only made it all the stranger.

"Over here, civsec."

He could still feel the eyes stabbing into the back of his head as he approached a small guard post at the other end of the hallway. This marked the third gate he had gone through; presumably every gate opened the way to inmates who had committed more and more serious crimes. Once he passed, he noticed that the guard accompanying him was gone. Turning around, he found him standing at the entrance.

"This is as far as I go. Be careful, civsec. That guy used his handcuffs to put me in a chokehold the first day he was here. If help came any later than it did, I would've been strangled."

"...All right. Thanks."

The guard bowed down to him, as if shrinking back in fear. Rentaro turned around, crossed the large C BLOCK stencil painted on the floor, and stepped into the darkness. He didn't exactly want to go it alone, but there was no way he could make the guard join him now. He wiped his sweaty palms on his pants.

This block was generally built like all the others, but the eyes upon him seemed to stick more closely to him than before, infused with a vague yet clearly murderous animosity.

Suddenly, there was a jangling sound from somewhere, like someone rolled a jingle bell along the floor. He followed the sound, which came from the far end of the corridor.

When he approached it, the first thing that struck him was the brightness. It was a single cell, a bit larger than the rest, and it had a window much larger than elsewhere, illuminating almost all of the cell's bare mortar walls. They loomed over a plain pipe-frame bed and a simple shelf lined with books, their titles written in Cyrillic. His attention then turned to the wind chime tied to one of the bars. The wind blew at it now and again, sending a bell jangling along inside its glass compartment every time it did. That must have been it.

And there, sitting in a folding chair and reading a book, was—

Rentaro made a pair of tight fists as he felt his blood vessels constrict.

"It's been a while, Andrei Litvintsev."

The man wedged a bookmark in his book, put it on the shelf next to him, and looked up.

"It sure has, Rentaro Satomi."

The tenor of his voice evoked unpleasant memories in Rentaro's mind.

He had a cleft chin and a well-chiseled face, one that didn't go too well with his black prison uniform. His blond hair shone in the sunlight. The tracking anklet on his right foot personified the sense of terror he projected, the same one the guard spoke of.

"Why did you ask for me?" Rentaro asked.

"I've been looking into you since my arrest."

Litvintsev tilted his head, inviting Rentaro to have a seat. Rentaro picked up a folding chair propped against the corridor wall and set it up for himself, never taking his eyes off his adversary. He made sure to leave three paces' worth of space between himself and the iron-bar door that separated them, just in case.

The chime jingled sweetly in the air, a sound heavily out of place in the oppressive atmosphere.

"First Scorpion, then Aldebaran... You've been busy since you caught me, haven't you?"

"You didn't bring me here just to crack jokes at me, I imagine. You sure got it good here, huh? Three hots and a cot, and all that."

"Wanna trade places?"

"Hey, I'm just saying, be glad you didn't get the death penalty."

Litvintsev's lips curled into a smile. "You don't have to be so nervous. I'm not gonna kill you or anything."

"I'm sorry, has your time in jail hurt your eyesight or something?"

The prisoner sneered a jeer of supreme confidence. "Fear has a certain scent to it. You're masking that fear with your anger right now."

"..."

Rentaro glared back, fists on his legs, as he kept himself from trembling. As much as he hated to admit it, he was never any good at playing mind games with people.

This was Andrei Litvintsev. A spy who gave bribes to several Tokyo Area politicians and tried convincing them to switch over to warmongering extremist groups. He was accused of building connections to the Area's heavy industrial, economic, and political powers, then reporting his findings back to Russia. He even built an operational office inside Tokyo Area for his activities.

The authorities finally caught up with him, but when they did, they were only able to arrest five other people connected to him. All exercised their right to remain silent, so the courts weren't able to pin anything on him apart from the meandering offense of "disturbing the peace in Tokyo Area and collusion with other nations."

It was sheer coincidence that a master spy like this was arrested at all. He was installing a litany of bugging devices in the house of a politician that opposed his friends, and the noise from the construction work annoyed one of the neighbors. That neighbor employed a civsec in order to file a complaint, and soon his entire cover was blown.

Litvintsev was the darling of the news media for a while after his arrest as his other crimes came to light—but to the Tendo Civil Security Agency, which had the limelight taken from them by the district attorney and was only involved in the first place because they were handling a dinky little noise-complaint job, it was a little embarrassing, if anything.

"The only reason you managed to catch me was because I didn't have an Initiator by my side. I don't want you to forget that."

"Heh. Pretty lame excuse. That's the kind of explanation an elite-level agent like you's turning to? Almost makes me wanna cry. Or should I say *ex*–elite agent?"

"Is that princess of yours doing well?"

"Lady Seitenshi, you mean? Was she in here?"

"Just for a little bit. Looked like a pretty delicate woman."

"Well, don't pick on her too much. She's a really devout woman."

"Devout?" Litvintsev asked, lowering his voice an octave or two. "She's turning to religion in times like these?"

"Are they all atheists over in Belarus?"

"Sorry. I stopped practicing once the Greater Minsk Area got thrown into the deepest pit of hell."

"…Look, Litvintsev, you know what's going on in Tokyo Area right now. The Area's been falsely accused of making Libra do its bidding. We're half a second away from war with Sendai. They're looking for a fight, in fact, and unless something happens soon, they're gonna get it—and once that happens, it might wind up being a world war. Now, there's a chance the things your people stole—Solomon's Ring and Scorpion's Neck—are involved with this. You were up to your neck in that, too, weren't you?"

"Why do you think that?"

"You're paying off the staff here so you can contact the outside world. That'd be easy for you, wouldn't it?"

Litvintsev chuckled as he shook his head.

"If you tell me where those people are now, I can negotiate to have your sentence reduced. And just so we're clear—if you don't give me some intel soon, don't be surprised if it's worthless for you later. I'm not as patient as you are."

Rentaro paused, gauging the response from the other man. Negotiations like these were largely unexplored terrain for him, but still he thought he did at least a tolerable job sounding caustic enough.

The Seitenshi had given him advance permission to promise Litvintsev a release if the need arose, on the condition that he'd be deported to Russia and forbidden from entering the five Areas of Japan again, but it'd be foolish in man-to-man negotiations like these to show your cards right at the outset. He was a dropout, yes, but Rentaro was once a military cadet during his years with the Tendo family, and he had a grip of the fundamental rules here, at least.

The regulations around this prison were strict to the point of paranoia. Only one visitation was allowed per month—even then limited only to family—and visitors were heavily restricted in what items they could bring into cells. Inmates weren't allowed to speak in the cafeteria, a place that served as the main social outpost for most other prisons. The ceiling was lined with tear-gas sprays set to deploy whenever any disturbance took place. Roll call took place twelve times per day; if you failed to respond, you were treated as an escapee and thrown into solitary. Even the twice-a-week outdoor recreation period, the lone chance inmates had to breathe fresh air, took place in an area surrounded by high concrete walls, patrolled by guards with live-ammunition rifles who circled above the prisoners like buzzards.

There was, in other words, no chance to relax for a single moment. It sickened most inmates. Many tried to escape, but there was no report of any successful attempts.

The strong defenses that lurked under the battered-looking exterior were symbolized by the extreme security measures taken in all areas. It was said that even the most hardened of thieves, killers, and arsonists broke down and cried like babies when told they were coming here.

Litvintsev may be acting tranquil, but half a year in this facility must be taking its toll. That was the conclusion Rentaro had made when he profiled Litvintsev beforehand. It meant Rentaro was the one dangling the fishing pole in front of him; there was no need for easy compromises. He just had to put the carrot in his face, then keep reeling it away.

The logical part of his mind knew that anyway, but on another dimension, his temples were throbbing with a sense of abject dread. There was no sense that the man in front of him could be driven by quick impulses. *Is that just an act? Or am I missing something fundamental, something decisive in my thoughts...?*

Litvintsev let out a snicker that, after a few seconds, changed to a louder, more ridiculing laugh.

"What's so funny?" Rentaro demanded. The prisoner glared back.

"I think you're misunderstanding something. I have no intention of negotiating with you."

"Wha...?!"

Rentaro couldn't believe his ears. *What did he just say…?*

He found himself lost for words as Litvintsev continued, "Now yes, I know I told that government official that I wanted to see you. That wasn't a lie, either. But I didn't call you here because I wanted to negotiate."

"So, what, then…?" Rentaro muttered in a raspy voice.

Litvintsev stood up and walked toward him. Rentaro knew the iron bars were there, but he still instinctively tilted his head back, steeling himself.

"Listen," Litvintsev said sternly, face against the bars. "Starting now, I am going to destroy both Tokyo and Sendai Areas. The people you love in your life are going to kill one another. They'll be blown to pieces. They'll have their guts splattered all over the pavement like a bug on the sole of your shoe. And you can't do anything except grit your teeth and watch, cursing yourself for being so powerless."

For a moment, Rentaro felt like he and Litvintsev had switched sides around the bars. The light from the window illuminated the prisoner's body only from the neck down; his head was completely dark, but his staring eyes shone brightly from within. They overpowered Rentaro, immobilizing him. But even in his paralyzed mind, one corner of his thoughts could understand the truth. His expectations had been completely overturned.

This wasn't a negotiation. It was a declaration of war.

"You better take your family and get out of this Area as soon as you can. I'm telling you this out of respect. You caught me once, so I owe you that much. But if you ignore this warning, you'll have to face a hell that's even worse than death."

"Don't give me that shit!"

Upon realizing that he could still move his arms, Rentaro immediately unholstered his handgun and pointed it between Litvintsev's eyes. The sight of the muzzle right in front of him put the prisoner into an eerie silence, his eyes stabbing at Rentaro.

"Why? Why would you do something like that?! Are you controlling Libra because you want Tokyo Area to taste what happened to your homeland? Why?!"

"You caught me once. But I'm not going to lose to you again."

A harried voice shouted out. Before Rentaro could comprehend it, someone rammed into his side, clouding his vision. By the time he realized it was a guard forcing his way between them, another had stripped the gun away and put him in a full nelson. He tried to resist the guards but stopped after they twisted his neck, incapacitating him in dull pain.

Litvintsev simply looked on, eyes frozen.

Damn it. Rentaro groaned as he was dragged away. *He had me in the palm of his hand. Here I am, thinking I'm reigning supreme, taking the leadership role in this chat—how could I be so stupid?* That vague gut feeling he'd had about the guy before he had met him—that had been correct the whole time. He was like a natural enemy—someone he should've killed the moment their eyes met.

After being chewed out by the guards and kicked out of the prison, Rentaro found himself awash in waves of inferiority. He dragged his body up, braving the intense fatigue as he traversed the wharf. Taking a look back, he glanced up at the bright sun, accompanied by the ever-chattering seagulls.

With a sigh, he began to wonder how Enju was doing in school.

3

The sound of Ms. Yagara's voice as she took attendance seemed to drone on and on like a mantra. The wide-bodied teacher seemed fully defeated by the day's humid weather.

"Hozui Watanabe... Um, right. Next, the girls. Enju Aihara... Er, Aihara?"

Momoka Hieda, alert upon hearing that name, stole a look three seats down. The seat was empty, her friend nowhere to be seen.

The sounds of the waves seemed to cleanse her head as she listened to the seagulls and closed her eyes, the light sound of water flowing nearly to the trunk of the knotted beech tree that her back leaned up against.

Swishing her legs to enjoy the feel of the grass against them, Enju Aihara took in the sight of the faraway buildings across Tokyo Bay.

The evaporating seawater made the offshore prison moored to the long wharf seem to shimmer in the air.

I wonder how Rentaro is doing with that prisoner. He happened to mention the location to her, so she decided to abandon school and head over to the nearby beach park.

Reaching into a bag, she took out a sandwich she had purchased at a convenience store along the way. Removing the plastic, she took a bite from one edge and swallowed. Now used to eating with her classmates, a solitary lunch seemed dull by comparison.

Just then, she turned her face up at the sound of a shrill voice. A family of three was enjoying a beach outing—at a time like this, no less. A mother and father were smiling awkwardly as a girl, their daughter presumably, pulled at their hands and shouted, "Come onnnn, let's gooooo!" The parents may have wanted a relaxing trip to the park, but their child, too inured to social games and other, more exciting entertainment, must've found it incredibly boring.

It was a happy family scene, one that should've warmed anyone's heart—but to Enju, it was discomforting. She was born as one of the Cursed Children, with no place in the world to call hers, and it was hard for her to look at a girl raised under the love of two parents and not take it personally. Normally she didn't even think about it, but whenever she felt battered down like this, even a teeny little trigger could break the seal on all the painful memories in her mind.

The first thing that sprang to her ears was the sharp sound of someone striking her. It was just a memory replayed in her head, but it seemed so real that she physically tensed up. There they were, two figures grinning at her swollen cheeks. The unforgettable Aihara family, her mother and father.

They never liked talking to her much. They preferred to express themselves through physical abuse instead. They starved her, made her sleep in the kitchen—they didn't want her; they wanted the stipend the government offered for adopting war orphans.

She recalled the way Sumire put it a while back: *"When you start attaching a monetary value to good intentions, you absolutely can't price it too high—or too low, either. For example, blood donation is so valuable precisely because it's meant as a donation. If you price it too low, people would see it as beneath them and stay away, but if it's too high, you'd start to see underground operations trying to profit off it. The late first Seitenshi is widely respected as a wise and able leader, but even she made at least one policy mistake. What was it? It was pricing the monthly benefit too high for taking in orphans."*

The Seitenshi must have gone into that with good intentions, but in the end it led to hyenas like the Aihara family appearing, licking their lips as they took in girls like Enju. Without love, of course no one could ever be a good parent. As long as Enju was breathing, they were satisfied. All other aspects of handling her eventually boiled down to either starving or punching her.

Of course, it didn't last.

She recalled herself standing in the living room, panting for breath. The dirty tatami-mat floor had been thoroughly destroyed. Her father, dressed only in a pair of boxers, was unconscious on the floor, his cheekbone practically caved in. Her walruslike mother, punched in similar fashion, was furtively edging away from her.

Her eyes were glowing a sheer red, blood dripping from each solid fist. She was pretty sure she was crying at the time. She had spent the past year trying everything to make them love her, but all the wishing in the world didn't get her that prize. Now, her relationship with her adoptive parents had finally crossed the line.

"It's—it's over for you!" her mother screeched at her as she bared her teeth, snapping Enju back to reality. "You're gonna be branded as dangerous and they'll get rid of you! I hope you're happy now!"

Stricken by terror, Enju fled. She wound up in District 39, where she kept herself alive by performing almost any crime one could think of apart from murder. It put her in danger of being shot on more than one occasion.

The care facility Enju lived in before the Aiharas took her knew that she was Cursed. They had long ostracized her, hoping she'd get out of there as soon as possible. There was no way she'd be allowed back.

Along the way, her eyes had started to harden. Scared of the ill intentions of those around her, she began to live with her abilities unleashed at all times. She stopped believing in people.

Somewhere along the line, another one of the Cursed told her that if she became an Initiator, they'd give her medicine to control her corrosion rate and wouldn't ever have to worry about where her next meal was coming from. She tried to volunteer, more testing it out than anything else—and while she could admit it now, there was something about the "Promoter" role, someone to guide and support her, that she was even looking forward to a little.

The sorrowful, hangdog-looking face on the Promoter that the IISO official linked her with, however, made her want to curse the heavens. And the face wasn't the worst part. He acted like some street hoodlum, and he barely had two pennies to rub against each other. Between him and the agency president, who looked as if most of the nutrients in her body were being used to support her voluminous boobs, she swore she'd never get along with either of them.

Enju took a big bite out of the sandwich in her hand. Why did she have to remember something like *that* at this point? Probably because Rentaro mentioned the Aihara family for the first time in a while over dinner last night. It was a sad connection for her—they gave her nothing but her last name—and now here she was, running again. First from her adoptive parents, and now from her classmates.

"It's so gross. Their eyes light up red, don't they? Why can't they just leave this school alone?"

"Why do they let 'em out of the ghetto at all?"

"They should stop pretending to be people. It makes me sick!"

All their words replayed in her mind, accompanied by their hateful expressions. She had eyelids that kept her from seeing the things she didn't want to, in theory at least, but she had nothing to plug up her ears.

It was a sharp, inarticulate "Agh!" from nearby that lifted Enju from her pit of self-loathing. She craned her neck to find a girl, younger than she was, staring up at an adjacent beech tree and looking about ready to bawl. Following her eyes upward, Enju quickly found out why. A bright red balloon, its string no longer held by anyone, was caught on the tree's branches, liable to break free and into the wide-open sky at any moment. The tree, at a good four meters or so, was too tall even for a grown-up to summit.

"Do you need that balloon?" Enju asked as she approached. The child looked timid at first but nodded after a moment.

Enju looked at her surroundings. For a single moment, nobody else was around—she could do it, but it'd have to be right now.

"Close your eyes for a minute."

"Close my eyes? Why?"

The question mark was practically visible over her head, but she meekly followed Enju's instructions.

"Keep them closed, okay?"

Enju closed her own eyes, focused on the center point of her body, and took a deep breath. With a single exhale, she unleashed her powers in one fell swoop. Her body grew lighter, as if gravity was starting to taper off, and her arms and legs felt longer as she enjoyed the feeling of omnipotence.

Crouching down to keep the girl from suspecting her, she leaped. Buoyed by the feeling of being pushed upward, she opened her eyes to find the red helium balloon right in front of her face.

Easily grabbing it, she went back down and patted the girl on the shoulder. She opened her eyes, a little reluctantly at first. There were many ways to describe how she reacted to the balloon provided to her—confusion, surprise, wonder, joy. Just watching her face vault between all the emotions filled Enju with happiness.

"Thank you, lady!"

Enju gave her a proud nod. "You're right! I'm totally a proper lady!"

The girl smiled back, although she didn't know what Enju meant. Her mother chose that moment to run up to them, bowing thankfully and chiding the girl for letting go of the balloon before taking her away.

The child waved at Enju several times as she walked off. Enju watched, reflecting on how doing a good deed for someone always made one feel great afterward.

"Are you one of the Cursed Children?"

The question made her spin a lightning-fast 180 degrees. There was another girl there, this one about the same age as Enju. Her silvery hair reflected the sunlight, and her black skirt and ruffled white blouse made her look stereotypically rich. Her unique ice-blue eyes gave her an intellectual air.

Enju froze, cold sweat running down. *She saw me?* An adult discovering her in her Cursed state would cause a huge uproar, a gaggle of onlookers, and God knew what after that.

"Wait just a second," the girl said, her cold eyes keeping Enju from turning around and running off. She covered her eyes with her right hand, then drew it away. Her ice-blue eyes were now a shade of dark ruby, shining amid the daylight. Enju gasped.

"You too?"

The girl nodded, put her hand up again, and removed it. Her eyes were back to their original shade.

"I wasn't expecting to see somebody like me here, so close to the Monoliths." She was about to raise a hand to salute Enju but stopped. "What are you doing here, though?"

"What about you...?" Enju stammered. It wouldn't do to reveal her current boycott of school. The girl looked down on the floor, her motives apparently just as difficult to discuss frankly.

Just as the conversation looked doomed to end, it was interrupted by a low, long rumble. The silver-haired girl grabbed her stomach, her cheeks blushing.

"That looks pretty good," she said, her eyes on the half-eaten sandwich in Enju's hand.

Ten minutes later, the girl and Enju were sitting on a shaded bench, the girl with a steaming fish-shaped *taiyaki* sweet cake in her hand. She gave the sweet a long hard look.

"The batter looks like it's made out of wheat flour, but there isn't really any fish inside, is there?"

"You've never had one before?"

The girl meekly shook her head.

"Well, it's got *anko* inside. Sweet red bean paste. It's good!"

"Oh," the girl replied. Then her brows fell, as if she was regretful of something. "But what about the money...?"

"Ah, it's my treat."

The girl still looked fiendishly conflicted about the *taiyaki*. Her body was less dishonest, releasing a single drop of saliva from the corner of her lips. That was enough of a trigger. She turned to Enju and gave a deep bow.

"Thank you for this. You really didn't need to feed me. This is my fault anyway. I didn't bring any extra money for today's activities."

"Activities?"

The girl opened her mouth and took a big bite instead of answering.

"Oh," Enju tried to warn, "it'll be hot, so you should take it slow instead of..."

"—?!"

The subsequent reaction from the girl was nothing short of intense. She squirmed on the bench, both hands covering her mouth.

"Hey! Spit it out! C'mon!"

"Ih...ih's nah haht 't all..."

"No, but..."

"...Ih's nah haht 't all!" the girl practically shouted, as if trying to convince herself. Her teary eyes suggested otherwise. She rolled the bite of *taiyaki* around in her mouth for a bit but finally managed to get a couple of decent chews on it before swallowing.

"B-besides," she added as she began to blow excessively on the rest of the treat, "I don't want to waste this after you gave it to me and everything."

Once bitten, twice shy, Enju thought as the girl timidly brought it back to her lips.

"Ah," she said solemnly as she enjoyed another bite. "I see. This works nicely, doesn't it? I burned the inside of my mouth too much to feel how it tastes, but..."

The sight made Enju laugh. She was about to call her by name until she remembered that she never asked it.

"My name's Enju. Enju Aihara. What's yours?"

The girl stopped just as she was about to take another extra-large bite, then thought for a moment before raising her eyebrows apologetically.

"I'm sorry, Enju. I'm afraid I can't tell you right now. Or I guess I should say that I don't want to, since if I told you, it might put you in trouble."

Don't want to...? It took a little while for Enju to understand what that meant.

"What does that...?"

The girl looked up at the clock mounted in the middle of the park. "Well, it's just about time. This might be good, actually. Enju, would you mind if I took a little of your time?"

The light-red sun set the sea ablaze in color as it slowly tilted its way westward. It was already too dark to see below the water's surface.

There was a sense of having no escape, coupled with a difficult-to-describe feeling of excitement. Enju reached out to the warm water's surface and put a finger to her lips. The salt stimulated her tongue, burning her throat on the way down.

The ripples lapped up and down along the boat's hull, making little splashing sounds as it bobbed the vessel this way and that. The distance from the boat to the shoreline was becoming unnerving to Enju.

"Are you sure we're okay here by ourselves?"

"No problem at all."

The silver-haired girl Enju was sharing the boat with gave her an assuaging smile as she kept pumping the oars. They were facing each other, and while the girl seemed to be looking right at Enju, her focus was actually on the area behind her back. Her eyes were red, her powers released; she must've been too afraid of someone at the beachfront park noticing them to keep them that way back there.

The two were out in Tokyo Bay, and Enju was starting to regret being so impulsive. She had been led to a dock where the girl had a boat hidden, and when she told her to hop on, Enju wound up doing so without really understanding what was going on. It was a tiny little thing, more suited for a tranquil pond than the wide-open sea—and they were alone on it, two children. If a fishing boat or cruise ship passed by, it might just land them in the news.

"Could you tell me why we're all the way out here already, please?"

"Because I wanted to be with you, Enju," the girl said with a half smile. Enju sat there, wondering what that meant. Even she could tell this wasn't the truth. With a sigh, she turned her ears toward the waves. A steam whistle went off somewhere. She decided to change the subject as she noticed the setting sun.

"Listen... What do you think about Cursed Children going to school with normal people?"

"Why are you asking me that?"

It was hard for Enju to explain. She decided to give the whole story—her origins; the one time her secret was revealed at school; the way her memories were dragging her down at her current one; her self-hatred at being dishonest with her own school friends. As she did, she couldn't help but wonder why she was revealing all this to a girl she had only met that day. If there was someone Cursed in her life she could open up to, it ought to have been Tina, not this girl.

The girl listened intently. When Enju was done, she closed her eyes, then opened them after a few moments.

"I'm sorry, Enju. I don't think I can really give you an effective solution to your problems."

Enju grinned and shook her head. "Ah, just listening to me... And not laughing at me, either. That's all I needed. I'm glad I did it."

"My homeland was already gone by the time I was born."

This startled Enju. The girl stood up as she looked at her, turning to a flock of seagulls, her eyes focused off in the distance.

"I lost mine in the Gastrea War. I was actually born in a neighboring country, but that country was rife with famine and discrimination. It was hard to live in."

A pause.

"The more you live in poverty, the more it makes you closer to an animal. You just eat, sleep, and produce offspring. Did you know, Enju? They did a study, and they found there's more than a ten-point difference in IQ between people who grew up hand-to-mouth and those who didn't. Supposedly your IQ goes back once things get better for you, but once you're in poverty, it's hard to gain the knowledge you need to claw your way out. That's what makes it so pernicious. Myself, I was lucky. I got picked up by someone and I lived in a pretty upper-class housing situation, but escaping that yoke—the three core desires of any living thing—made me realize that thinking, and reasoning, really is the only thing separating us from other animals."

She turned around, holding her hair down against the wind.

"I don't know if that really compares to your problems, but whenever things get hard for you, I think you should remember that. How you aren't the only one who has issues in their life."

Is it really right, though, using that as a support—that there are people worse off than you? That's simply looking down on them, isn't it?

The girl, perhaps reading Enju's mind based off her expression, gently shook her head.

"I mean, the connections we make with other people, Enju, no matter how annoying they can be sometimes, form the net that helps you break up and absorb the sad or difficult things that happen in your life. There's nothing shameful about taking advantage of that when you need to."

Enju felt that her closed heart had suddenly grown lighter, that the setting sun looked a notch brighter than before. She looked at her palms, balling them into fists and releasing them.

"It's weird," she said. "I don't feel as gloomy."

"It's an honor to help you," the girl said, narrowing her eyes with a smile.

"You're a really nice girl," Enju replied, giving her a smile of her own. "You should come to my place, so I can introduce my Promoter to you. We're madly in love—he barely even lets me sleep at night, even!"

"Oh? I'm glad to hear you have a good Promoter, too."

"Is yours nice?"

"Oh, very much so," the girl said, beaming as if she was the one who had received the compliment. It made Enju wonder who this girl was all over again. Given her pale white skin and silver hair, she must have been a non-Japanese Initiator, at least. They came to Tokyo Area a lot, Enju had heard, whenever some issue related to Varanium rights popped up. She wouldn't know, though. It wasn't like Initiators always revealed their abilities freely to one another.

"Well," Enju blithely noted, "I bet you're a pretty good Initiator. Strong, too. Able to make the right decisions all the time."

The girl scowled a bit at this appraisal. "Oh, not at all, no," she said in a dejected tone before falling silent and pretending to focus on rowing the boat.

Enju brought her body up, worried she had touched upon something she shouldn't have—then a pang of pain crossed her head. Looking around, she immediately saw why. There were two gigantic walls of jet-black Varanium in front of her, one on each side. She had taken care to scope out the beachfront first and stick to an area between the Monoliths where the Varanium force was at its weakest. This boat must have taken her to a point beyond what was safe for maintaining her equilibrium.

"Are you all right?" Enju asked.

"I think I am, yes. It's hurting you at this distance? You must be pretty sensitive. Forgive me if I'm being rude, Enju, but what is your corrosion rate?"

"Around 25.4 percent, I think. You?"

"Fairly close to that, yes." The girl looked at Enju, perplexed. "It's strange, though. If our rates are nearly the same, we should be equally affected by the Varanium fields, too."

"Oh, really?"

Come to think of it, Tina had about the same corrosion rate, too, and it was the same deal with her. Enju figured her body was just more sensitive to Varanium than the norm.

"Well," the girl concluded, "maybe it's related to your genetic makeup or something. Ah, we've arrived."

Enju looked around. There was nothing near them they could have moored to.

"I needed to visit that building over there," the girl said, pointing to the landing point as she pulled out a pair of binoculars. It was starting to grow dark, and even without the visual aid, Enju could see the offshore prison looming far larger than before.

"You've got something to do in this prison, too?"

The girl's eyes opened up wide. "Well! That's a surprise. I didn't think you'd know that was a prison." She looked at her watch, then threw herself down, lowering her center of gravity as she kept the binoculars in hand.

"They'll be here in a second."

As Enju puzzled over this, she spotted the presence of a boat advancing upon them from the side. She lowered her own head as well. It was about as large as a fishing vessel, and it passed them by without paying their boat any special attention. Once it passed, though, it made a wide turn and approached the prison from the rear, mooring at the Mega-Float's small loading dock.

"There's a network of naval mines around the area to keep prisoners from escaping, and the guards can set them off from land if they want to. The ship's taking the longer route in order to avoid them. They must be shipping something over that's too difficult to carry by land."

The girl beckoned Enju to come next to her, then handed her the binoculars.

"Very tight security, indeed. Can you see, Enju? It looks like just another weather-beaten building, but it's packed with all the latest technology—sensors, biometric authentication, you name it. The walls look like they're falling apart, but I heard they're reinforced with Varanium core material, so they can probably take a real beating."

The girl was too focused on her excited commentary to notice the expression on her conversational partner.

"Um, so why are you scoping out a prison?"

The girl flashed a look of guilt before averting her eyes. "Oh, I'm just a fan of prisons like these..."

Enju shot a perplexed look at her suddenly taciturn partner. Presumably, the girl would have arrived here even if they hadn't met—and yet, when she ran into Enju, the girl was dead set on her coming along. Maybe she was just being used to fill up the ranks, since two people on a little recreational boat ride would draw less attention than a solitary rower in the bay. Enju should've been angered by being used like this, but she couldn't drum up the reaction.

To be honest, she was starting to like this mystery girl quite a bit. She recalled Rentaro telling her that if she found someone she wanted to be friends with her whole life, she needed to treat them well, no matter what.

"I guess there's a reason why you can't tell anyone else. I won't pry, I promise."

The girl furrowed her brows. "Thank you, Enju, but...we should probably head back. Sorry to ferry you all around the bay like this."

The seagulls above them cried out into the evening as the dwindling sunlight colored the girl's face red.

"Do you think we could meet again?"

"I think it'd be better for both of us," replied the girl, "if we didn't." She gave an inscrutable smile. "My name is Yulia."

"Huh?"

She ran a hand through the hair above her ears. "I said, my name is Yulia Kochenkova."

4

"Yulia Kochenkova," the Seitenshi said as she looked at the photograph that popped up. "Andrei Litvintsev's Initiator; the strongest of the former Belarus region. She was once a member of Witch Squadron, a special-forces unit manned exclusively by Initiators. Her Gastrea factor is the cheetah."

It was past seven in the evening at Rentaro Satomi's darkened apartment. The crystal in the middle of it shone blue, just like it had the day before, as it projected a holographic window into space. Rentaro tapped the photo, expanding it out. The girl, in what looked like a hidden-camera photo, was turned toward the left, lips pulled tight in an off-putting expression.

"Cheetah...?"

"Yes. Oriented for speed. The same type of Initiator as Enju, in other words."

Rentaro whistled in astonishment. The cheetah required no introduction. It was the fastest hunter in the animal kingdom, clocking speeds upward of 110 kilometers an hour. An Initiator's strength in battle was far from wholly dependent on their animal-based Gastrea element. *But*, Rentaro thought, *if it's a cheetah we're talking about, that's practically a thoroughbred among Initiators.*

"What's her IP Rank?"

The Seitenshi paused for a moment before reluctantly blurting out the number. Rentaro reacted by rubbing his arms nervously, a chill coming over him. If that number was for real, this might turn out to be the toughest job assignment he'd ever taken.

"You haven't run into her before, have you, Mr. Satomi?"

"If we had run into her half a year ago," Rentaro said, embittered, "Enju and I would be dead right now."

The Seitenshi fell silent at this statement, taking a sip of tea from the low table. "Ten years ago," she said, "when Belarus was by and large obliterated by the viruses released by the King of Plagues, Yulia Kochenkova's mother just barely managed to flee to Russia safely. She gave birth to her at a refugee camp set up by the Russian government, but she died soon after from a postpartum infection and fever. Any well-equipped medical facility would have been able to save her life, but that just didn't exist at the time."

"...How are Cursed Children treated in Russia?"

"About as bad as it gets," came the melancholy reply. "Moscow Area is the largest colony in Russia, and they agreed to take in all refugees without any restrictions, leading to a severe financial crunch that affected the lives of all Russians. That, to say the least, led to discontent. Rumors went around that the Belarusians were all infected with delayed-action viruses from the King of Plagues.

"This ultimately led to a sort of caste system put in place across Russia after the war. Refugees from Greater Minsk were the low rung on the ladder, and among them, the Cursed Children—they're literally called the House of Witches in Russian—are barely even treated as human. They were almost wiped out from the region entirely before the Russians realized the threat from outside Gastrea and formed the Witch Squadron to fight them. Kochenkova was lucky to still be alive when she joined them. She was found curled up in some alleyway, eating rotten food, and she didn't even have the strength to bat away the flies around her face."

The Seitenshi closed her eyes. Rentaro had known her long enough to understand what she was thinking. She was at it again—feeling personal sympathy, personal pain for the plight of people she had no chance on earth of saving. He didn't see that as a waste of time per se, but in her position, he thought, it was important to pick her battles.

She continued her silence. Was she just being stubborn? Or was she truly as holy as the aura she portrayed, still searching in the darkness for a better answer to the problems Rentaro had resigned himself to abandoning long ago?

"So?" he asked, breaking his chain of thought. "What happened then?"

"She received a high level of education in the squadron, something she still feels an enormous debt of gratitude for. Reportedly she met Litvintsev around the same time."

The Seitenshi turned toward Rentaro.

"Mr. Satomi, if you don't mind me asking about your gut feeling on this... How did you do with Litvintsev?"

"He's definitely pulling the strings." Rentaro bit his lip as he recalled the previous afternoon. "He's a dangerous man, and he's sharp as a knife, too."

Damn it all. There's so little time left, too.

Then Rentaro noticed something warm on top of the clenched fists over his knees. Surprised, he looked up to find the Seitenshi, in all her pale beauty, right next to him. He swiveled his eyes back down, only to find her smooth, velvety long gloves covering his own hands.

"This hasn't ended yet. We need to place our hopes on tomorrow."

"Y-yeah..."

Rentaro found himself reflexively rearing back at the sight of the beautiful, snowlike face, the glossy lips, just a few centimeters from his body. Her breath, the breath of a woman who a rich real-estate developer once reportedly expressed a desire to spend his entire fortune on a pair of lace gloves for, was beating against his neck.

This situation—the two alone in a man's apartment with only the crystal's erratic illumination to light them—was probably something he should have been better prepared for. He gave her a look. "What is it, Mr. Satomi?" she replied innocently.

He turned back toward the photo of Yulia, racked with guilt from the assorted unpleasant situations his mind conjured up.

"...So we're basically one hundred percent sure she's in Tokyo Area, right?"

"Her current whereabouts are unknown. She managed to evade our investigators, and I'm sure it'll be all but impossible to get a bead on her again."

The lights went back on, the crystal automatically turning off in response.

"I'm back!"

Turning around, Rentaro found Enju at the light switch, removing her shoes by the front door.

"I made a new Initiator friend today. You wanna hear about her?"

Rentaro waved his hand in front of his face. After their conversation just now, he preferred not to think about Initiators for a while to come.

"Welcome back, Enju," the Seitenshi said graciously.

"Why's Lady Seitenshi acting like a newlywed wife around you, Rentaro?"

"Huh?"

"Rentaro," she angrily continued, "I want my customary welcome-back peck on the cheek."

"We never do that."

This made Enju jump up and down indignantly. "I don't care! I wanna kiss!"

Why she was choosing this hill to make her last stand on, Rentaro had to wonder as he tossed Enju into the bathroom and made her wash her hands and gargle.

"I'm gonna skip school tomorrow, Rentaro," she said, sticking her head out the doorway with a cup in her hand, "so I can help you find the terrorists, okay?"

"You've got school tomorrow?" Rentaro asked. He had just gotten word that Magata High School was giving students the day off tomorrow, in light of the whole King of Plagues scare.

"Yeah. They're going on a field trip to some power plant in the Outer Districts. The teacher said it didn't see any action during the Third Kanto Battle, so it won't get caught up in a war this time, either, so..."

This exasperated Rentaro. *What a place I got Enju into,* he thought to himself. But then he realized this could be a good chance for him.

"Yeah, you go to school tomorrow, Enju. You just got into it; you oughta take every chance you have to get into the swing of things. You don't have to worry about us."

"But isn't there gonna be a war if we don't...?"

Rentaro patted Enju a few times on the head. "It's fine. If I need your help, I promise I'll contact you."

She nodded, albeit with some reservations.

Enju's already had two schools taken from her, Rentaro thought. *I won't let it happen a third time.*

5

The ocean wind running between the iron bars set off the wind chime again.

From within the eternal darkness surrounding the moon, the sound of the waves continued incessantly, and the sharp scent in the air seemed to attach itself to everything that it found.

It was past lights-out time, and Andrei Litvintsev's eyes were closed as he sat on his bed and counted the number of wave crashes. In the single cell across from his, a large man with an eerily porcine body lay sound asleep. He had the sleeves on his prison outfit rolled up and he unconsciously scratched his stomach as he snored. Other people, in other cells, could be heard either weeping or muttering to themselves.

It made Litvintsev feel like he was traversing the space between dreams and reality. There was no telling how much time he spent in this state.

Suddenly, he heard a single word—*Captain*—in the air. Slowly, he opened his eyes, only to find another pair illuminated in the darkness on the other side of the bars. And it wasn't alone—there were others behind it, although they were trying to hide themselves.

"You're right on time."

He stood up and walked to the iron-bar door. The electronic lock was disengaged, as if by magic, and with quiet footsteps Litvintsev's late-night visitors crammed into the cramped cell. Among them were five men and two young women.

"Great to see you again, Captain," a man in a balaclava and full tactical gear said, almost overcome with emotion. Litvintsev knew him. The other men followed his lead, removing their masks and saluting.

Litvintsev nodded and sized up each one individually.

"Max, Misha...and Sonia, too, eh? Great to see all of you. Where's Yulia?"

"Right here."

Another girl entered the dark cell. Her silvery hair and ice-blue eyes reflected the moonlight as she stood bolt upright and gave a brisk salute. After she put her hand down, her face twisted, grimacing, and she hugged Litvintsev's midsection, burying her face in his side.

"I've wanted to see you for so long, Captain."

"Everything going well?"

"Exactly as you commanded." Remembering her role in the current mission, Yulia took a step back and kneeled. "I'm off to support our people occupying the monitor control room."

She stood back up, turned around, and soundlessly disappeared. In her place, the man Litvintsev had identified as Max stepped forward and saluted.

"We need you to prepare to leave in twenty seconds, sir. Your escape ship is waiting out back. We'll be detected any moment now."

As if on cue, a shrill alarm cut through the night. The sleeping prisoners jumped to their feet, yelling confusedly at one another.

"Speak of the devil," observed Max as he replaced his balaclava and removed the safety on his rifle. "Please hurry, sir. We're here to guide you out of here. We have the Neck and the Ring for you, too. You'll have a front-row seat for the final events."

Another member of the team provided Litvintsev with his favorite coat to wear over his uniform. He sized them all up one more time.

"Okay. We've been wanting this long enough. Let's do it."

They moved out in perfect sync—Litvintsev's people taking the lead with rifles slung over their shoulders, the rescued prisoner coursing through the wind behind them.

The prison, forced awake by the alarm, was transformed into a whirlwind of chaos. The bars that should have slapped upward from the floor to prevent escapes never deployed. No contact was made with authorities outside the prison. And the guards who headed for the monitor control room after the alarm went off were more than a bit surprised by the hail of bullets that greeted them there.

The gunshots thundered across the whole facility, sparking off the steel desks used as impromptu barriers.

"Get back!" one of the guards shouted over the furor. "That's a professional team that's taken over the control room! We can't beat 'em with our equipment!"

One of his coworkers found a free moment to jump over the barricade and fire a volley with his shotgun. He immediately threw himself back down after a swarm of bullets was sent his way. "Damn it," he growled.

It went without saying that the prison guards were not professionally trained soldiers. They had a modicum of firepower, mostly meant for riot suppression, but asking them to take on a clearly sophisticated squadron of well-supplied fighters was beyond their abilities.

Just as they were trying to figure out what to do, they realized the gunfire had stopped. One of them looked up to scope out the room.

Just as he did, a masked man tossed something out from behind his barricade. The guard froze as he observed the circular object—a fragmentation grenade. He drew his head back, anticipating the intense pain about to greet him.

There was the sound of something hitting against metal, followed by an explosion. A shockwave struck any body parts not hidden behind the barricade. Dust filled the air as bits of plaster blew off the walls.

"Get out of here! You're too weak!"

Am I alive? The man honestly wasn't sure when he opened his eyes. There he saw the back of a compactly framed young girl. She stood there wielding a pair of Varanium cutlasses, each one about sixty centimeters long.

She whirled around at the stunned guard, earrings spinning in the air. There was a spade mark painted under her right eye.

"Oh! The Initiator!"

The girl grunted sullenly at him. "Ritsu Urabe, Initiator Rank 550. You—get out of here and call for backup. I'll take care of these guys."

Few of the guards appreciated the presence of an Initiator among their ranks before, but—as they discovered now—she had just kicked the grenade away from them. It put the guards in a daze.

"Uh, okay. Be careful. There's two of them stationed in front of the control room."

The guard gave Ritsu a pat on the shoulder before running off. She watched him go, then turned toward the door. She grinned at the barricade, teeth grinding, as she spotted something moving behind it. The next moment, a barrage of muzzle flashes was quickly followed by a mass of bullets.

Ritsu, reading it perfectly, jumped away. Amid the insane rush of gunfire, she dashed to and fro, slashing right through the barricade once she reached it. The look of sheer shock on the face of the enemy soldier behind it was exactly the kind of thing she savored in life. She gave him no time to regroup, burying her fist in his collar. He screamed and dropped his rifle.

Then her animal instincts told her to jump. She did so, and a rifle bolt pierced through the air she had occupied a second earlier, sending concrete pieces flying as it embedded itself in the wall.

"You picked the wrong girl to mess with!"

She flipped her body and kicked off the ceiling, falling toward the armed enemy and slashing diagonally with both swords when she landed. The Varanium blades easily sliced through the body armor, neatly placing the soldier out of the picture.

"Gr...ahh..."

The skirmish was over. The masked man fell to his knees, gushing blood as he looked up, mortified, at his attacker.

Ritsu licked her lips in excited anticipation. There was nothing she liked more than seeing this—taking those who underestimated her and making them crawl away in pain.

"I'm not gonna kill you yet," she said. "I got a ton of things I wanna ask you."

She turned around to visit the control room. Then, sensing another threat, she turned around again. From the other end of the corridor, a girl appeared.

She had silver hair, ice-blue eyes, and a khaki military uniform. In another place and time, one might think she was just a tiny little girl who had gotten separated from her parents.

However, this was neither that place nor that time. The enemy terrorists must have had an Initiator on their side, too.

The silver-haired newcomer eyed her downed comrades, then nodded in understanding. She knew what needed to be done. It was Initiator against Initiator; no need to exchange words. Both knew this wouldn't end until blood was spilled.

But as the girl stalked her prey, Ritsu couldn't help but speak up.

"What's up with that? You're actually gonna fight with those things?"

She had on a pair of knuckle guards, a metal pole attached to each arm with four long claws per hand and rings to put her thumb through. It was a pair of *bagh naka*, *tiger claws*, made for assassins to give their victim deep stab and claw wounds, as if they were attacked by a vicious animal.

Ritsu was dubious. They were Varanium, yes, and lightweight enough to keep the user agile, but they had essentially no reach. They were a relic from a past era.

"Ritsu Urabe, Initiator Rank 550. Model Shark."

The girl bowed respectfully in reply.

A moment later:

"...What?"

The girl raised an eyebrow, wondering if Ritsu didn't hear her. Then she lowered herself, ready for combat. Her eyes looked straight ahead.

"I *said*, Yulia Kochenkova, Model Cheetah. Initiator Rank 77. This is over."

6

He didn't bother asking for change as he threw a wad of cash at the cabbie before flying out of the car. It was brighter outside than he'd expected, forcing him to shade his eyes. It was cold, but the eastern sun had already risen. The waves made soothing sounds, something they'd no doubt be doing a thousand years from now.

By comparison, the offshore prison had undergone some major transformations since his last visit yesterday. There was now a tinge of blood to the salty sea breeze. He could feel his body tense up.

As he ran across the long wharf, he began to see a large number of onlookers jostling for position, along with the police officers trying to keep them away. "Hey, no entry—" a guard shouted at Rentaro. He stopped midsentence once Rentaro took his civsec license out and tossed it at him.

The elderly guard looked at it, then made a face at him. "You guys horning in on our territory again? This ain't no Gastrea job."

"But there's a chance an Initiator was involved with this, right? That oughta give me the right to go in."

"Pfft…"

The guard rolled his eyes as he lifted the police tape for Rentaro. "Show me who's in charge of the scene," he asked. The guard motioned for him to follow and started walking.

He took advantage of this invitation to scope out the rather noisy surroundings. This artificial island usually housed nothing but prisoners, guards, and their families; now it was full of forensics guys, local police, even a few special-forces men. In a way, one could describe it as a festival-like atmosphere, although not a very happy one.

Underneath the crape myrtle flowers that blossomed by the outer walls, there were a few red spider lilies strutting their stuff, a bold crimson color as they rocked in the wind. There was no telling where their seeds could've flown in from. Nearby, Rentaro could see blood spatters, human figures outlined in tape on the floor, and a seemingly infinite number of bullet holes.

"That tape… Which side were they on?"

"I dunno."

The scene inside the prison was even uglier than the one outside.

On their way in, Rentaro passed by the SAT (Special Assault Team), all decked out in bulletproof gear, assault rifles, light machine guns, and more. Fatigue was written all over their faces; they must not have gotten any sleep since their overnight deployment.

After that, Rentaro passed a guard prodding a handcuffed prisoner down the hall. The prisoner alternated between muttering to himself and cursing at the guard as he stubbornly held his ground for as long as he could.

"Move it!" the guard shouted, running past Rentaro's elderly guide just as they reached the large door that led to the monitor control room. The remains of some barricades were nearby, indicating that combat must've happened here as well.

There was a small crowd in front of the door. Rentaro saluted them, and then the forensics crew, decked out in jumpsuits and identifying armbands, cleared the way for him.

That brought the girl on the floor into view.

"..."

The field of psychology tells us that people use clothing to appeal to others, to adjust how they want to look to the world around them. It was clear that the girl sprawled out at Rentaro's feet wanted people to know that she considered herself a rebel. One could imagine a career in punk rock for her, cameras flashing nonstop as she surfed over a crowd of passionate, screaming fans. *She* had probably imagined it, too.

Along those lines, her dream had come true. The "camera flashing" part, at least, although the cameras belonged to the police crime-scene unit instead of some entertainment outlet.

The direct cause of death, Rentaro presumed, was shock brought on by the slashing claw wound to her abdomen. The strike had plucked out a great deal of her innards, making sickening red designs on the floor. The wound, which looked like it was administered by a grizzly bear, left much of her stomach cavity open for the world to observe.

She was looking straight at Rentaro now, eyes still full of surprise. Chances were, she didn't have enough time to comprehend what had happened to her before the end came.

"Ritsu Urabe. She's an Initiator, IP Rank number 550."

Rentaro turned around to find a plainclothes police detective in short sleeves addressing him. He had a square jaw, black hair that was graying in spots, and black-framed glasses that gave him an intellectual look, although his thick eyebrows suggested an equally strong will beneath the smarts.

"You running the scene, sir?"

"I'm the one. Yoshitatsu Akutsu, superintendent."

He took a cigarette out of his chest pocket and lit it up.

"Uh, you shouldn't be smoking at a crime scene."

"Ah, lay off. I wouldn't be able to stand this stench unless I masked it with something stronger... Hey, we're done here, right? Let's send 'er on her way!"

He motioned to the crime-scene officials, who had just finished taping up the girl's outlines on the floor. They responded by loading her on a stretcher, putting a white cloth over her, and carrying her off.

There wasn't much of a physical resemblance, but the aura Superintendent Akutsu presented to Rentaro reminded him a lot of Detective Tadashima, his old acquaintance. Probably just as stubborn and in the trenches as Tadashima, too, he thought. And once Rentaro was sure of that, he knew exactly how to deal with him.

"Do you really need to bother with doing up the entire crime scene like this, sir?"

"We gotta make it clear who killed who before anything else. Sentencing gets to be a pain in the ass if you skip that part."

"Oh. Makes sense." Rentaro turned to Akutsu. "Has the riot been stopped?"

Akutsu shut his eyes for a bit, blowing tobacco smoke from both nostrils.

"More or less."

The news all but horrified Rentaro this morning. Last night, a riot had broken out at the offshore prison, leading to the escape of no less than three hundred and eighty inmates. They had taken a hundred and twenty people hostage, including the guards who didn't make it out in time and their families who lived on the Mega-Float; they'd managed to take over the entire island for a period of time. They asked for a ransom and safe passage out of Tokyo Area, and promised to shoot one hostage dead every hour that passed beyond their deadline, although the time they gave was clearly not enough to satisfy their demands.

They followed through with their threat, taking their first victim once the deadline came along, despite the efforts of police negotiators. Eyewitnesses talked to the media about the despair, spreading like a disease across the hostages' faces, when the news went around.

"I'm impressed you got things under control in less than half a day."

"Don't thank me. Save the compliments for our SAT teams on the ground. They swam their way through the minefield, entered through the prison's back entrance, and took control of the prison's monitor control room. There they activated the tear-gas sprays across the entire prison and synced that with their assault from the front door."

Akutsu blew some smoke into the air, deep lines around his eyes.

"We lost a few of the hostages, sadly, but that was the whole reason why speed was so important. Even as it is, we're running into some serious shortages in beds and free prison cells."

"Any SAT casualties?"

"None at all, they said."

Rentaro was astonished. "Talk about some real pros."

Akutsu gave him a look. "Oh, like *you're* one to talk. You subdued an entire team of SAT officers barehanded back at the Magata Plaza Hotel, didn't you? I mean, that's not even human, man. You know? Some 'Hero of Tokyo Area' you are."

Rentaro had been about to take out his license, but it turned out there was no need for that.

"So you know me?"

"Of course I do. And just in case you didn't know, there's, oh, a thousand guys in police headquarters who'd love to kill you right now. Our HR situation is a complete mess, thanks to you taking down Commissioner Hitsuma and all those other managers. I'm supposed to be a superintendent, but I'm having to do police-chief duties on the side, too. To hell with that shit. I wanna be out on the streets, not behind some creaky old desk."

"Well, keep it up, and I'll make you commissioner before too long."

"Oh, God, anything but that," Akutsu said, grinning as he waved his hands at him.

"So, was there someone named Andrei Litvintsev among the dead or injured prisoners?"

"Nope," the superintendent said, "no one like that. There *might* be a chance he's still hiding out on the island somewhere, but I sincerely doubt it. According to the prisoners we interrogated, he went out of his cell with a whole group of people and pretty much immediately vanished."

Akutsu flipped open his notebook, bringing it up to his horn rims so that it was practically touching.

"Other prisoners witnessed a single motorboat roaring away from this island. They wired the minefield behind the prison so they could set it off whenever they wanted, but if nothing went boom out there, I'd say our suspects somehow got their hands on the safe route out to sea."

"Well, yeah. The first thing they did was take over the control room and turn off all the security. They definitely did their homework."

Akutsu scratched his head in aggravation. "Damn it. Why does this have to happen *just* before we're gonna go to war or somethin' with Sendai Area?"

If only he knew how related those two things were.

"Um," a voice said from behind. Rentaro turned around to find a younger officer, looking a bit agitated as he fiddled with the brim of his hat.

"Are you Rentaro Satomi? There's a woman here to see you."

Oh, now what? Rentaro tsked to himself. *This isn't the time.*

"Tell her I'm busy."

"I told her several times that this was authorized-personnel only, but she refuses to listen to me, and"—the officer hesitated for a moment—"I didn't get a good look at her face because she's got the hood up on her outfit, but she's really beautiful. Like, elegant, or something. So I had a really hard time saying no to her, but…"

Rentaro's temples throbbed. He didn't like where this was going at all. He zoomed around to find someone jumping up and down among the throngs behind the police tape, waving frantically.

"Mr. Satomi! It's me!"

He brought a hand to his face. "Get over here," he shouted, raising the tape and grabbing the girl's hand. A few moments later, they were in a more secluded area on the island, behind the prison itself.

"What the hell are you *doing* here?"

The girl pulled down her hood, revealing her clear, pale skin and snow-white hair shining keenly in the sunlight. It couldn't have been anyone but the Seitenshi.

"I couldn't allow myself to merely sit alone in your home while you were running about, trying to handle my request. I know I can help you, Mr. Satomi. Besides, my disguise is perfect."

The Seitenshi spun around in place, and the bottom of her skirt lifted into the air as if floating. She was wearing a collared white dress with a white jacket and a pair of white boots to tie the outfit together. Smiling, she lowered the jacket's light hood.

She was, in a word, beautiful.

Any annoyance Rentaro felt at her presence was instantly banished as the beauty, indescribable by mere words, floored him. He realized he had never seen her in anything other than her formal palace dress. As a full-fledged public figure, she wore that outfit every waking hour of her life; it was another way to inform her citizens that she was in their service.

Seeing her do away with that, even for disguise purposes, indicated to Rentaro that something deep within the Seitenshi had changed. He wondered if he was improper to think it.

Realizing she had stunned him into silence, the Seitenshi timidly lowered her head. But her eyes looked up, toward his, as if begging for something.

"Does it…look good on me?"

Rentaro turned his back to her.

"Uh, if you're gonna disguise yourself, try picking one that won't make ten out of ten men passing by try to ask you out."

The Seitenshi blushed, bowing her head even farther.

"Oh, Mr. Satomi, are you…?"

Just before things got even more awkward, three crime-scene handlers arrived from around the corner of the opposite building, chatting with one another. The Seitenshi hurriedly put her hood back on.

Rentaro breathed a sigh of relief. Then he realized she was looking right at the group of chatting men.

"I'm impressed the police force is still functioning as normal. There might be war tomorrow, for all we know. I suppose we owe that to Kikunojo's managerial skills."

Rentaro sized up the group. "Nah," he rebutted. "Disaster experts call it *normalcy bias*."

She looked up at him with large, questioning eyes. "Normalcy bias?"

"Yeah. When someone's facing an upcoming disaster, it's hard to make them pull the switch that says 'Hey, this is really bad, we need to do something.' People can be surprisingly lazy like that. Plus, if everyone around you's acting normal and you're the only one freaking out, people find that embarrassing. Even if there's a hot iron right at your feet, a lot of people can't make themselves take action at all."

"I think people were a lot more on edge during the Third Kanto Battle, though…"

"Well, that's because everyone knows that a Monolith falling down spells instant annihilation for all of us. The Gastrea War was only ten years ago, and we've had a handful of Pandemics since then, so everyone in the Area's used to the evacuation drills by now. But the last time people fought against one another in large-scale combat here in Japan was in World War II, back in 1945. Pretty much everyone who experienced that for themselves is dead, so none of us are capable of imagining what'll happen next. They're probably thinking something like, 'Well, maybe it won't be as bad as a Pandemic, at least.'"

The Seitenshi despondently narrowed her eyes. "Oh, but it could wind up so much worse, though…"

Rentaro crossed his arms. "The real problem," he observed, "is over in Sendai Area. Like, things are a lot more urgent for them, because they're seriously in danger of being wiped off the map. I wish I knew what Ino was gonna do next…"

"Hey! Guys!" a man shouted to the trio on the other side, running up to them. "Check out the TV! It's crazy!"

The trio exchanged looks, nodded, and followed the newcomer. Rentaro turned to the woman beside him. She was already gazing at him.

"We should go, too."

They entered the prison, following closely behind the trio as they filed into the cafeteria. There was a single LCD TV attached to one wall of the cavernous chamber, assorted police detectives and crime-scene officials fanned around it in a crowd. They all watched the screen with bated breath, the air tense. Rentaro had to stand on his toes to get a look.

A chill ran down his spine.

The screen showed a gigantic centipedal Gastrea, one that made the bare rock surrounding it look like a miniature set. Its face was reptilian, and its legs, outfitted with scythelike serrated blades, seemed to be nearly infinite in number.

It was Libra, the King of Plagues. But what shocked Rentaro wasn't the sight of Libra itself; it was the translucent viral sacs around its stomach area. They were inflated and taut, like party balloons, and they jiggled around, seemingly ready to release their lethal payload at any moment.

Rentaro wiped sweaty palms on his pants legs.

The scene changed to what was presumably file footage of Ino holding a press conference. The content was nothing if not predictable. The prime minister shook his fist in the air, his speech too loud and anger laden to make out clearly. Among what Rentaro could make out, however: *"If Tokyo Area does not withdraw Libra by three a.m. tomorrow, we will launch a simultaneous full-scale attack on both Libra and Tokyo."*

The officers around the TV nervously chattered with one another as the screen returned to the news studio, an anchorman warning viewers to stay away from private weapon manufacturers, self-defense force facilities, and other locations likely to be Sendai Area's initial targets. He then moved on to a primer on basic anti-disaster preparations.

Rentaro gingerly turned to his side. The Seitenshi, head under the hood, watched the screen sternly.

"Before I fled the palace, I asked them to send a diplomat over to Sendai Area, but...by the looks of things, I doubt they're making much progress."

She turned toward him.

"Mr. Satomi, did you notice? Prime Minister Ino may have been incensed, but he did not act like an insane man. He sounded rational to me. Despite how bellicose they're being with their speeches, wouldn't it be safe to say that Sendai Area is still hesitating to go through with it? Isn't this their way of telling anyone who noticed that they're willing to wait up until the very last moment?"

Rentaro silently admired her for making that observation. She hadn't become head of a nation out of pure happenstance, after all.

After a while, once the TV news started repeating itself, the Seitenshi shrugged, her face exhausted. "Would it be all right if I rested over there?" she said, pointing to a corner of the cafeteria.

Taking a chair and following her, Rentaro couldn't help but notice that despite the early-morning hour, there was an oddly spicy scent coming from the kitchen.

"I'm sure the cafeteria staff must be making breakfast for all the police who spent the night handling the riot," observed the Seitenshi. "I'll go see if we can get some, too."

She stood up before he could stop her and talked things over with one of the cooks, who bowed deeply to her. "Here you go," she said as she carried two trays back, each with a plate of rice curry. Never in Rentaro's life did he ever imagine the most powerful person in his homeland running waitress duties for him. He wondered what her servants in the palace would think about that as he took in the warm, inviting curry aroma, the spices stimulating his sense of smell in an extremely pleasant fashion.

Although not too enthusiastic about it at first, he picked up a spoonful and brought it to his mouth. Then his eyes shot wide open. It was a perfect harmony—sweet, spicy, and just the right amount of salt. The sensation of the melt-in-your-mouth curry, accompanied by the onions and potatoes in the sauce, made him drown in euphoria. He wasn't even really thinking about food before the plate arrived, but the next thing he knew, he was taking one spoonful after another, trying to get at every grain of rice.

On the other side of the table, though, there was the Seitenshi, spoon in hand, just staring at her own steaming plate.

"What is it?" he asked.

"No, I…I mean, my meals in the palace were managed for an exact balance of vitamins and nutrients down to the last milligram, so…I was just thinking what they'd say if they saw this."

"Lady, you're the head of state. You can eat whatever you want."

The Seitenshi quietly shook her head. "Not quite. I may be head of state, but that does not put me in a ruling position over my people. I speak for the people who selected me, and I have a duty to give them everything I have."

She closed her eyes, bringing a hand to her cheek.

"I am blessed, it is true, to receive a great deal of compliments on my appearance. People, for better or worse, seek beauty from me, and if beauty helps my voice come across more clearly to my people, then I would gladly consider my body, too, to be in their service. That is why I strive for beauty, and if I disrupt my nutritional balance, that could cause my beauty to disappear, breaking the unwritten law between myself and my— *Mmph!*"

Rentaro used the hand that wasn't shoving a spoonful of curry in her mouth to rub one of his shoulders. Just listening to her go on was making them ache.

The Seitenshi shot to her feet, shaking with surprise. "Wh-what are you doing?! I—I... Not even my own mother ever did something as brazen as—"

"—It's impolite to talk with your mouth full."

It was only then that she realized she hadn't so much as chewed yet. She covered her mouth, blushing, as she swallowed. Now her eyes were filled with a more pleasant sort of surprise.

"...This is good."

"Yeah, isn't it? Isn't that the whole point? If it's good, who cares? As long as you're with me, at least, forget about all that 'head of state' crap. If you can't, then get your ass back in the palace now."

"Y...es. You're right... Thank you, Mr. Satomi."

The Seitenshi gave him a warm, bright smile, so bright that Rentaro couldn't stand to look at it with the naked eye. Something about the pickled relish the curry came with seemed particularly bittersweet to him, now that he was eating it to hide his embarrassment.

The two fell into an amicable if slightly awkward silence after that, opting to concentrate on their meals instead of idle conversation. It was the Seitenshi who finally broke the ice again.

"You've made your rounds around the prison, right, Mr. Satomi?"

"Yeah. Looks like Litvintsev fled on us."

"Did you notice anything else, though?"

Rentaro's spoon halted in midair before reaching his mouth.

"There's one thing that's bothering me, yeah. There was a dead Initiator sprawled out in front of the control room. She was sent out from the IISO on security detail; Rank 550. Done in by that Kochenkova girl, the one you warned me about yesterday."

"Are you sure about that?"

"We're talking about someone who could kill Rank 550 in one strike."

Rentaro recalled the tigerlike claw wound as well as the death mask of surprise on the victim's face. He shook his head. "They got us... They really got us. This Yulia Kochenkova girl—I know she's way more powerful than Enju. I swear, that's one Initiator I could never let her fight..."

"Mr. Satomi, I've been thinking about Litvintsev a little myself, and I've been wondering: Why did he take the risk of calling you over if he knew he was going to escape the very next day?"

"..."

"Because here's my idea. I'm thinking that he wanted to give you a personal message before he left. Something along the lines of...well, 'Catch me if you can,' I suppose."

Bitter, Rentaro crossed his arms, rubbing them with both hands and gritting his teeth. *Are you saying you can make the entire world shudder all by yourself? You, a single person?* He had to be honest with himself—he didn't want to get involved with that man ever again. Just seeing the full strength of Yulia in action turned him off the idea for good.

If he kept pursuing Litvintsev, he felt instinctively it'd lead to events that he'd likely regret for the rest of his life. This was, after all, the Russian military he was dealing with. Each one of them a trained professional. Cold-blooded pros who wouldn't flinch at murder for the sake of their mission. They lived in a different world.

But, at the same time, he also knew that there was no turning back. If he didn't take action, after all, it would affect the lives of an unimaginably huge number of people.

"This fight isn't over yet, Mr. Satomi. Let's rack our brains and figure out where Litvintsev might be hiding."

Rentaro heaved a sigh and tried to keep his mind serene. "Yeah," he said. "Let's start by thinking about where Litvintsev and his crew could have gone."

The Seitenshi gave him a soft smile. "I'd be glad to help."

It didn't matter to him if this was just a brave show she was putting on. He silently ordered himself to think about the future instead as he sat back in his seat and crossed his arms.

"Okay, so do you have any ideas, even rough ones, of where they're hiding out? They couldn't have fled Tokyo Area *that* quickly."

"That's what I thought, too. Even if the hull of their motorboat was lined with Varanium, that wouldn't be enough to engage seafaring Gastrea. I would guess they're hiding out in Tokyo Area after getting back on land."

"Could they have taken a plane out of the Area?"

"Tokyo Area's air defenses are on high alert with the whole Sendai Area threat. They wouldn't let a single gnat escape the Area right now. There's a nonzero chance, I suppose, but I think we'd be safe to ignore it."

Rentaro carefully took his thoughts one step further. "You explained to me a couple days ago that Litvintsev's people were using Solomon's Ring and the Scorpion's Neck to take control of Libra."

"Right. Stage Fives can communicate with one another via sound and electrical waves, so they might be stimulating the vocal cords taken from Scorpion's corpse to create those waves. Then they could use the Ring as a translator to exchange messages. To put it another way, they could use the Neck to convince Libra that Scorpion is still alive."

"But how are they getting those signals or whatever all the way to Mount Nasu in Tochigi Prefecture? That's over one hundred and fifty kilometers away as the crow flies. I don't know anything about wave physics or whatever, but can you send an electrical signal that far without it falling apart?"

"The answer to that is right above your head, Mr. Satomi."

Rentaro followed the Seitenshi's pointed finger up to the stained, faded ceiling. A line of tear-gas sprayers was situated directly above. *That probably wasn't what she meant*, Rentaro figured. But then it finally struck him:

"Oh! A satellite...?"

The Seitenshi nodded approvingly. "Good. That was some fast thinking, Mr. Satomi. Geosynchronous satellites are generally equipped with relay devices called transponders. A site on Earth's surface can send a signal up to one, and the transponder will amplify the signal and send it back to another site. That essentially eliminates any physical wave-strength limitations, and I'm sure that's what Litvintsev and his men are using."

"Well...wait. Hang on." Rentaro raised a hand to stop her as he attempted to collate his disparate thoughts. "Aren't satellites expensive? It's not like everyone's allowed to use them."

"Exactly. As of 2031, most satellite access is restricted to police, civil security, or military usage. Someplace like Shiba Heavy Weapons launching a satellite of their own is the exception to the rule, really. I don't know if your mobile phone can work via satellite access or not, Mr. Satomi, but if it does, you have the right to own that only because of your civsec license."

Rentaro nodded. A satellite phone, which by definition never found itself without service access, was a must for civsecs active in places like the Unexplored Territory. Agents like him had permission to use them, as well as military-grade GPS tracking technology.

"Is satellite bandwidth or whatever still that precious these days?"

"Yes. Geosynchronous satellites have a shelf life of five to fifteen years, so they have to be relaunched on regular occasions. The Gastrea War, however, cost most nations the entirety of their space programs. Sagittarius shot down a lot of them during the War, too..."

"Oh...right," Rentaro said, a sour taste in his mouth.

"So it's fair to say that wherever Litvintsev and his team are hiding, it's got to have a satellite uplink and downlink on premises. That'll narrow our list of candidates pretty quickly."

"An uplink and a downlink? Is that like sending and receiving data from a satellite?"

"Right, right."

"Kind of like uploading and downloading, huh?"

The Seitenshi frowned a little, finger on her chin. "Um, not really, is it?"

Rentaro dropped the topic instead of letting it slow their progress. "So, uh, how many places in Tokyo Area would have that kind of up- and downlink capability?"

"One."

"Huh?" Rentaro asked incredulously. "So that's gotta be the place, right?"

"No," the Seitenshi said as she solemnly shook her head. "Not there."

"What? But—"

"It couldn't possibly be there. That's why nobody in the palace is doing anything about it."

Now there was real force behind her voice. Force that would've made anyone hesitate to press on. If she was that insistent about it, Rentaro reasoned, it must have been safe to remove it from the list.

But—damn it, this was getting annoying. Anything he could've thought up with his feeble knowledge, the Seitenshi already considered a decade ago. *I guess this is the end of the road,* Rentaro thought. *So this is it? I'm doomed to just sit here and watch Litvintsev engineer all-out war between Tokyo and Sendai?*

Just as his mind was about to voyage into dark, murky waters, a helping hand arrived from an unlikely source.

"Oof!" uttered an elderly voice as something pushed Rentaro from the side. It was Superintendent Akutsu, sitting down at the table with a plate of curry in hand. The eyes buried in his wrinkled face swiveled over to his.

"Why're you guys helping yourself to the food they made for us, huh?" he growled. "And you've got your girl here, too? What the hell?"

The Seitenshi's chair clattered as she got up, face red as an apple as she struggled to say something.

"I...I...I am *not* Rentaro's 'girl,' good sir...!"

"Good what?"

She covered her mouth, brought the hood down over her head, and sat back down on the chair with a heavy thud.

"Wh-what do you want, though?" Rentaro asked, striving to get the conversation back on track.

"Could've sworn I heard that voice before...but anyway, you're trying to track down Litvintsev, aren't you?"

"Yeah."

Akutsu narrowed his eyes and let out a chiding laugh.

"Well, you're in luck, 'cause we got a witness here who might just know where he ran off to."

AFTERWORD

All the readers holding this book in their hands might feel a little dubious right now, wondering why this volume is rather surprisingly thin compared to previous ones. Considering the rest of the *Black Bullet* series always clocks in at around three hundred pages in the Japanese editions, I'm sure one can't help but notice that Volume 7... doesn't.

The original plan for this volume called for a story that could be contained in a single book, like Volume 2, since both the Volume 3/4 and Volume 5/6 pairs wound up being two-parters. However, thanks to some (ahem) issues with my writing speed, it was decided that we'd cut it off at the middle and publish it like this instead.

My sincere apologies go out to anyone expecting the usual length with this volume. There's no point dwelling on the past, however, so right now my sole focus is on making the second half as exciting as it can possibly be.

Now, about the manga version.

For the edition coming out in March, *Dengeki Maou* magazine is launching a second manga version of the *Black Bullet* series. Titled *Black Bullet Interlude FAQ!* it's a high-tension gag series (or so they tell me) penned by abua, an artist with a truly original sense of humor. Pick up a copy to check out the *Black Bullet* characters in all their screaming, shouting, bawling glory.

Finally, I'd like to hand out some thank-yous.

First, thanks to Kurosaki, my editor, who fought diligently to extend out the schedule as much as humanly possible. Thanks also to Saki Ukai, my illustrator, who performed some fairly amazing scheduling acrobatics in order to accommodate me as well. Hellos and kudos go out to Morinohon and abua, authors of the two *Black Bullet* manga versions, as well as everyone in the editorial and publishing teams involved in getting this out to market.

Also, one more word to my readers. By the time this reaches print,

I think the anime version will be just about underway. Personally, I think it'd be great if it turns into something that really wows all of you.

Thanks, as always, for picking up this volume. May the blessings of the gods fall upon everyone who lays eyes upon this.

Shiden Kanzaki

Congrats on the
anime version!
I'm so happy I'll get to see all
these crazy kids running
around on-screen soon!
Here's hoping all of you
check it out, too!

Saki Ukai

BLACK BULLET 1

MORINOHON
Original Story: SHIDEN KANZAKI
Character Design: SAKI UKAI

Translation: Nita Lieu
Lettering: Abigail Blackman

BLACK BULLET Volume 1
©SHIDEN KANZAKI/MORINOHON 2013
All rights reserved.
Edited by ASCII MEDIA WORKS
First published in Japan in 2013 by KADOKAWA CORPORATION, Tokyo.
English translation rights arranged with KADOKAWA CORPORATION, Tokyo,
through Tuttle-Mori Agency, Inc., Tokyo.

English translation © 2015 by Yen Press, LLC

Yen Press
1290 Avenue of the Americas
New York, NY 10104

Visit us at yenpress.com
facebook.com/yenpress
twitter.com/yenpress
yenpress.tumblr.com
instagram.com/yenpress

First Yen Press Edition: September 2015

Yen Press is an imprint of Yen Press, LLC.
The Yen Press name and logo are trademarks of Yen Press, LLC.

ISBN: 978-0-316-34503-3

Printed in the United States of America

I'LL BE THERE SOON.

OH, IT'S NOTHING, KOHINA.

I'M JUST A LITTLE PREOC- CUPIED.

ZA (SKSH)

WHA ...!?

JARI (KRNCH)

PI (BEEP)

PATAN (SNAP)

READ MORE IN *BLACK BULLET* MANGA VOLUME 1!

22

MM-HMM.

YEAH.

I SEE. OKAY.

PI

KOHINA ...?

PIRO (DING)

PIRO

PIRO

PIRO

PIRO

JAKA (KACHK)

!

OVER HERE, YOU MON- STER!

I'LL COME MEET UP WITH YOU NOW —

IDIO—

OOO (WHOO)

THIS IS FOR MY COM- RADES!

PAN (BANG)

DON'T COME IN RE—

GAAN
(BAM)

GNH!!

DO
GWHAM)

DAMN
...

PARA
(CRUMBLE)

PARA

SHUUUU
(FSHHH)

HEH.

PI
(BEEP)

ZA
(ZSH)

HFF!

HFF!

!

20

HEE HEE!

YOU'RE AWFULLY LATE, AREN'T YOU?

WHY DO I SAY THAT, YOU ASK...?

BUT I AM DECIDEDLY NOT IN THE SAME BUSINESS AS YOU.

IT'S TRUE THAT I TOO WAS AFTER THE GASTREA THAT WAS THE SOURCE OF THIS INFECTION.

HMM...

WHAT THE...? ARE YOU...

KA

KA (TAK)

0000

000

BECAUSE THE ONE WHO KILLED THOSE TWO POLICE OFFICERS...

...A CIVSEC OFFICER TOO?

...IS ME.

JAKON
(KACHAK)

OOO
(WHOOO)

CHAKI
(CHK)

TCH.

DAMN IT...

...DON'T GIVE ME MORE WORK TO DO. DON'T MAKE MY JOB EVEN HARDER.

DO IT.

I'M GONNA BREAK IT DOWN!

......

GASHA (KRRSH)

HEY.

KUI (FLICK)

WHA....!?

TCH.

SINCE THEN...

...WE HAVEN'T HAD ANY RESPONSE FROM THEM...

JUST A FEW MINUTES AGO, TWO OF OUR POINT MEN WENT IN THROUGH THE WINDOW.

THOSE GUYS... ALWAYS COMING ON THE SCENE AND MAKING A BIG SHOW OF IT...

WE DIDN'T WANT THEM STEALING THE CREDIT FROM US!

WHY DIDN'T YOU WAIT FOR CIVSEC TO ARRIVE!?

GA (GRAB)

YOU IDIOTS!

OUTTA THE WAY, YOU IDIOTS!

DON (SHOVE)

WHO CARES ABOUT THAT!?

MORE IM-POR-TANTLY—

YOU UNDER-STAND HOW THAT FEELS TOO, DON'T YOU, SIR!?

U-UH, WELL ...!

YOU CIVSEC OFFICERS FIGHT IN PAIRS, DON'T YOU?

HUH?

... WHERE'S ...

...YOUR INITIATOR PARTNER?

RAAA

RENTAR

I CAN'T GO OUT IF I'M NOT DRESSED PROPERLY!!

HEY! DON'T RUSH ME!

GEEZ, I SAID HURRY UP!

I DIDN'T THINK THE SITUATION WAS BAD ENOUGH THAT WE'D NEED HER!

DOOR

SHAKO (PEDAL)

SHAKO

SHAKO

GORO

GORO

GORO (ROLL)

WAIT

I'LL FALL ....!!

PREZ!? UH, YES, YES, RIGHT AWAY! WE'RE LEAVING NOW!!

W...

ANY CHANG-ES?

WELL...

HEY.

SIR!

!

KA (TAK)

MAYBE I SHOULDN'T HAVE LEFT HER...

10

NOT LONG AFTER MANKIND'S DEFEAT...

I'M THE ONE WHO SHOULD BE SAYING "GEEZ"...

......

CIV-SEC!

HURRY UP, AND GET OVER HERE!

...THE POLICE WEREN'T EXACTLY THRILLED ABOUT THE CIVIL OFFICERS WHO CROSSED THE LINE INTO POLICE JURISDICTION.

HOW-EVER...

...IN AN EFFORT TO REDUCE THE POLICE OFFICER FATALITY RATE...

...A LAW WAS PASSED THAT FORBIDS A POLICE OFFICER TO ENTER THE SCENE OF A GASTREA-RELATED CRIME WITHOUT A CIVIL SECURITY— "CIVSEC"— OFFICER.

THEY'VE SOME-HOW KEPT UP APPEARANCES REPEATING THIS UNPRODUCTIVE BACK-AND-FORTH TIME AFTER TIME.

ALL RIGHT, ALL RIGHT...

COME TO THINK OF IT...

HM?

カッ KA

カッ KA

カッ KA (TAK)

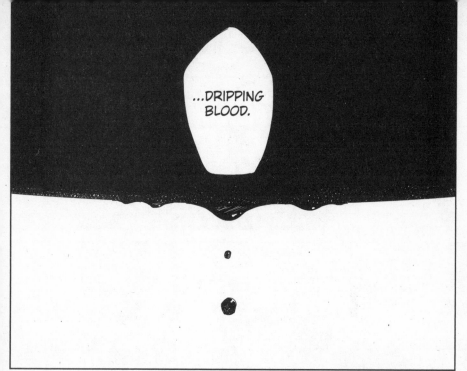

...DRIPPING
BLOOD.

ANYWAY,
YOU'LL
SEE ONCE
YOU GO
IN.

SO...

...PUTTING
ALL THE
EVIDENCE
TOGETHER,
THERE'S NO
DOUBT IT'S A
GASTREA.

I CAN
FINALLY
GO IN NOW
THAT CIVIL
SECURITY'S
SHOWED
UP.

GEEZ.

ZA

ZA
CZSH

THE INCIDENT OCCURRED ON THE SECOND FLOOR OF THIS APARTMENT BUILDING.

ZA- (SKFF)

OOOOOOO (WHOOOO)

"LEAK-ING"...?

A WATER LEAK?

YEAH.

TURNS OUT IT WAS...

SAID SOMETHING WAS LEAKING INTO HIS APARTMENT FROM THE ROOM ABOVE.

THE GUY IN ROOM 102 WAS HYSTERICAL WHEN HE CALLED.

6

A STRANGE VIRUS THAT APPEARED SUDDENLY AND SEIZED THE HUMAN POPULATION.

GAS-TREA.

ITS VICTIMS SOON OVERRAN THE WORLD WITH THEIR ASTOUNDING POWER...

THE VIRUS COULD SPREAD THROUGH BODILY FLUIDS...

...AND MANKIND'S POSITION AT THE TOP OF THE FOOD CHAIN WAS EASILY STOLEN.

...AND REWRITE A LIVING ORGANISM'S DNA, MAKING IT MUTATE INTO SOMETHING GROTESQUE.

TEN YEARS PASSED, AND IT IS NOW THE YEAR 2031.

CHAPTER 1　PROMOTER, INITIATOR

SPECIAL PREVIEW OF
BLACK BULLET VOL. II

THE YEAR 2021.

MANKIND LOST TO GASTREA.